1-11-05

SSLg

&F

& 01

L

& 05

DATE DUE

Western
Paine, Lauran.
Guns of the law /

PLEASE LEAVE
CARD IN POCKET

MAY   1999

Guns of the Law

Guns of the Law

LAURAN PAINE

Sagebrush
Large Print Westerns

Library of Congress Cataloging in Publication Data

Paine, Lauran.
    Guns of the law / Lauran Paine.
      p.   cm.
    ISBN 1-57490-173-7 (alk. paper)
    1. Large type books. I. Title.
[PS3566.A34G87 1999]
813'.54—dc21   98-48131
                                                                                      CIP

Cataloguing in Publication Data is available from
the British Library and the National Library of Australia.

Sagebrush Large Print Westerns are published in the United
States and Canada by Thomas T. Beeler, Publisher, Box 659,
Hampton Falls, New Hampshire 03844-0659. ISBN 1-57490-173-7

Published in the United Kingdom, Eire, and the Republic of South
Africa by Isis Publishing Ltd, 7 Centremead, Osney Mead, Oxford
OX2 0ES England. ISBN 0-7531-6001-3

Published in Australia and New Zealand by Australian Large Print
Audio & Video Pty Ltd, 17 Mohr Street, Tullamarine, Victoria, 3043,
Australia. ISBN 1-86442-267-X

Manufactured in the United States of America by BookCrafters, Inc.

Guns of the
Law

CHAPTER 1

HE HAD, OF COURSE, NO FURTHER WORK TO DO. THEY had caught the horse-thief and locked him up, the townsmen had gone home or to the saloon, and swift-falling summer night was closing down. Another day was finished and another job was done; the town's constable would patrol Gorman's Crossing—or just plain Gorman, as folks were calling the town now—and therefore he could go home.

But he didn't. He stood there, casting a sharp-edged shadow in the growing dusk, gazing off into space, allowing himself to drift back in time, back to the summer before.

At that time, the summer of 1878, the golden summer, he had been twenty-two years of age. He had just come to Arizona Territory with a wicked-horned herd of Panhandle cattle, and he hadn't been in Gorman's Crossing a week before he had encountered Carrie Lee Longstreet. And for him that was the end of everything that had gone before. The finish of the divergent directions his life might have taken. The snuffing out of a dream he'd entertained, since earliest boyhood, of having a ranch of his own.

He had danced with her at the Fourth of July celebration, and he had walked her through the grove of cottonwoods, and he had told her, "I could love you, Carrie Lee . . . No, I already do!"

For half that wonderful summer they were sweethearts. He had got a job as shotgun messenger on the stage, but that had kept him away too much, so he'd gone to work at the livery barn. She'd sniffed at that,

1

and perhaps he should have been warned, but he was twenty-two and that was a magical summer. There had never in his life been a summer like that one before; there never would be again . . .

The days had spun out in sparkling beauty and the nights were heart-hurting fragrance, and she had been a lodestar drawing him; a dazzling lodestar because she was lovely to look at, firm-fleshed, dark-eyed and dazzling, sought after by every rider in the country, eager to dance, anxious to smile. A little imperious perhaps, but bewitchingly so, maddeningly so.

That had been the summer of innocence, he thought now, standing in the dusk, and if he had been younger or different he could have wept for it: the loss of innocence. As it was, he stood there with his lips pushed together, feeling with unconscious effort the rise of heat from cracked earth, the pulse of night, dark-shadowed.

Those were the days a man couldn't keep, he could only cherish them in his heart. And they had ended badly, for late that summer Carrie Lee had urged him on to something better than the livery barn job. He'd worked for Emmon's Mercantile, but the pay was no better, and by then they were going to get married. She needed new clothes. He worked at the mercantile by day and the livery barn by night. But Old Man Smith, the liveryman, had come to him gently . . . then he'd had only the mercantile job. But they'd got married anyway.

Then he'd hired out to Sheriff Nat Hendrick, who was ten years his senior and in love himself, and while the pay was better it still wasn't enough.

A woman came slowly forward beneath the wooden overhang, and he turned. "Good evening, Russ," she said. "Is Nat inside?"

"'Evening, Betty. Yes, he's in there."

2

She went past, disappeared beyond the door of the sheriff's office, and Deputy Russ Bell drew himself up. Four bunched-up riders loped past, their jangle penetrating his mood. He watched them go south toward the saloon with a soft banner of laughter in their wake, then he turned north and started walking down the night.

Nat Hendrick was a saddle-warped thirty-two; his hands had large knuckles and, like his face, were deeply tanned from summer scorch. He wasn't above average height, but there was a depth of power in his thick compactness, and he was deceptively light and swift. When Betty Aldridge entered the office he was sitting at the desk with weary looseness. When he raised his head she could see the riding dust on him, and his eyes, lying on her, were dully introspective.

She knew how he felt; it was a hot summer, the air was leaden, with a scent of staleness to it, and he'd been on a chase. She'd seen him look like this before, all slack and gaunt-eyed with tiredness. "Did you get him, Nat?" she asked softly.

He nodded his head. "We got him. He's back there locked up. We got the horses back, too, all tucked up from thirst."

"I just saw Russ outside."

The direct gray glance clung to her face. "Just now? I thought he went home half an hour ago."

"He was standing out there in the shadows."

The sheriff pushed back and got up. There was something unfriendly and condemning in his voice when he said, "Yeah. I guess he would be, at that."

From beneath her lashes Betty could see the set expression of his face. She fingered the buckle of a limp shell-belt on the desk. "Has he said anything to you yet?"

3

"No, and he won't. Russ isn't the whining kind." The tired body turned, the gray eyes looked out hard and stone-set. "She's goin' to ruin him, Betty," Nat said. "She'll destroy everything he's got in him that a young feller should be able to keep . . . at least a few years longer."

"The baby will change her, Nat. Come on; I've got a big roast in the oven." She turned toward the door, and his hard gaze softened as she moved.

Outside darkness was down, black and full and only slightly relieved by a filling moon and the glitter of diamond-sharp stars. From over the way came the lift of carefree voices and the stab of bright lamplight upon the murky dust of the roadway from the Durelle Saloon. She waited while Nat spoke briefly with his nightman, his smoky glance running past to her unsmiling but alive. Then he came, and they walked by side, with the music of his spurs soft in the gloom.

The café was empty, and after they'd come in she drew the shade which showed the place was closed. She set a table while he scrubbed, and later they ate. "We could walk down there," she said.

"Not tonight, I'm not up to it. Besides . . He made a cigarette and lit it. "What can we do?"

"Maybe, like last time, Nat, we can interrupt a quarrel."

He regarded the top of his cigarette moodily. "Why aren't we like that?" he asked her softly, without looking up.

"We're different people. I've worked most of my life and so have you. Carrie Lee's never worked. When she was at home the ranch hands spoiled her. After her mother died she was the only light in her father's life. She's never had to struggle and she can't do it now."

"I'm paying Russ every nickel my budget'll allow. If

4

they can't make it on what he's making now, they'll never make it."

"It isn't the money, Nat."

He looked up, a dry crinkle up around his eyes. "No? She wants dresses, a driving buggy, someone to come in once a week and clean the house her paw gave them It's nothing *but* the money, Betty."

"I didn't mean it like that. I meant. . . love. I meant that she must have loved him or she wouldn't have married him. Love can get along on very little cash for a long time, Nat. Look at Bedelia and Charley."

"It's enough to scare a man out," he said, seeming not to hear her. "He was in the saddle under that boiling sun all day . . . when he gets home he gets a quarrel for supper."

Betty rose, got busy with the plates. "If you marry a plain woman," she said, "you won't have any of those things to worry about. The only thing a plain woman can offer is love."

Tiny lines showed at the outer corners of his eyes. He was loose and comfortable in the chair. "You're not plain, Betty. You're mature; there's a lot of woman to you. The thing about you is that you grow on a man."

"You mean my pot roasts do."

"Well, partly that." He got up heavily and watched her clear the table. "I like my women to have big feet and sturdy legs and—"

"My feet are *not* big!"

"Well, no, I didn't say yours, I said I like my women to have big feet—like a good saddle-horse has big feet—and sturdy legs. I don't want so much beauty, I want something durable and usable and—"

"Some day you're going to tease like this, Nat Hendrick, and I'm going to—"

5

He reached for her, drew her roughly to him. The beat of his breath was hard on her face, and the force of his will—and the hunger in him—was burned into her with his kiss. He was as aware of the pounding of his heart as she was, and as conscious of the hardening of his muscles. Then he moved back, and, because of the weakness in her legs, she put a hand behind her on the table, looking up at him. With the most solemn of looks he said, "That'll do for dessert, Betty," and she laughed in spite of the catch in her throat and the tumult deep inside. He was over by the door before she spoke.

"Nat? Did you hear about the Duncan robbery?"

"Yes. They told us out at Dorset's when we took the horses back. If they made their getaway in this direction I hope they go around town; I've got enough on my mind right now. Good night, Betty—you're the best cook on this side of the road." There was a Chinese café among the shanties of Gorman's west end and it was on the opposite side of the street. She drew herself up and he ducked out, closing the door with a hard pull after himself.

A soft tinkling of music lay in the night as he went west along the planking toward the saloon. It grew louder, less melodious and more frantic, the farther he progressed. A plump and elderly man accosted him, wearing a mirthless smile. "Sheriff, I've been looking for you."

"'Evening, Mr. Semple. What's the trouble?"

"Well now, Sheriff, it's not really trouble." Semple's round, smooth face glistened in the watery light. "It's just that Roscoe's a mite behind with his note at the bank, you see, and I thought maybe you could jog his memory a little about it."

"Roscoe," Nat said with careful enunciation, "is a man now, and aside from the fact that he wouldn't take

6

kindly to having me badger him for you, about the best way I know to get him orry-eyed is to call him Roscoe."

"Russ then," the banker said. "Well, you understand how things are, Sheriff. I don't want to embarrass him."

"How much does he owe you?"

"Not me, the bank. He owes two hundred dollars plus interest. Now, if he's a mite short and would just pay the interest, you see, why that'd make it easier . . ."

"How much is the interest, Mr. Semple?"

"Ten dollars."

Nat dug into a pocket, brought forth two crumpled bills and handed one to the banker. "There's your interest, Mr. Semple," he said in the same distinct tone. "When Russ comes around apply it to principal, or whatever bankers do, and don't let him know I paid it."

"All right, Sheriff, but the point is . . . things like this don't help the boy's standing, you know."

An odd expression settled over the sheriff's face. "Mr. Semple," he said softly, "how many men in this town would dig into their pockets to pay your interest, if you owed any?" He pushed past the banker and continued on his way. Semple saw him disappear through the doors of the Durelle Saloon. As Chairman of the Town Council of Gorman's Crossing, George Semple was not a good man for a county sheriff to antagonize.

The Durelle Saloon was a shag-scented room of barn-like dimensions. It was drafty in winter but cool in summer, and it never, summer or winter, day or night, lost its chest-high halo of tobacco smoke, nor its lucrative popularity. Other saloons had opened in Gorman's Crossing across the years, but Durelle's alone had survived; it was an institution, not only among cowboys, freighters and stagers, but also among merchants and cowmen. A popular story among

7

cowboys, that was bristlingly unpopular with Gorman's Crossing's merchants and townsmen, was that someday the name of the village would be changed to Durelle, Arizona Territory.

The sheriff was halfway through the noisy press of sweaty bodies when someone called his name over the bedlam. He turned. A large, florid man sitting alone at a wall table motioned to him with his head, and kicked out an empty chair. "Over here, Nat. Never mind the drink, I got a bottle here."

Nat worked his way over and sat down wagging his head. "Worse'n Saturday night," he said. The cowman poured a stiff drink and shoved the glass forward. Nat drank, put the glass down and sucked in a big lungful of stale air. "Thanks," he said. "How are you, John?"

"Well, I'm healthy," the cowman replied. "I came into town a-purpose to see you, Nat. Banged on the office door till Sheepy woke up and told me you weren't there, then I looked high an' low for you." The ruddy face thrust forward and massive shoulders hunched down. "You got Dorset's Slash HD horses back, I hear."

"Yeah; we got the horses and the thief," Nat replied, studying John Summer's craggy features. "You lose some, too?"

"Nope." The big cowman leaned back with his mouth drawn flat, and placed two large hands palms-down on the tabletop. "My trouble's a little different. You see, Nat, we been gathering out of the hills for about a week now getting ready to make the fall tally, and you know I've always saved that prairie grass west of the mountains for my holding ground."

"I know, John."

"Well, sir, a trail herd's camped there."

Nat scowled. "This time of year? Why, there isn't

8

enough green feed this side of Canada to keep cattle in flesh this time of year, John."

"I know that, dammit, but the point is they are there. Now, Nat, you know I'm a peaceable man and all . . ." The sheriff made a dubious grin which Summer chose not to see. "So I went an' talked to those fellers. They told me they'd come a long ways and didn't like to use up my feed, but that their critters had to rest for a few days."

"In other words," Nat said, "they wouldn't move."

"That's right."

"Where are your animals?"

"They're up there, too, but I got my hands stayin' with them to keep the two herds separated." Summer poured himself a drink, downed it and ground his teeth against the raw burn in his gullet. "Now, Nat, I'm not going to be pushed off my own range by absolute strangers, but before I do anything, I want your ideas."

The matter of free-range jurisdiction had always been a tough one. Actual ownership lay with the government, but local custom invariably recognized the oldest—and strongest—user, as having control. Nat gathered his legs under him and leaned forward to rise. Then he said, "John, you know where you stand as well as I do. The land isn't yours except by custom."

"It sure isn't *theirs*, Nat!"

"No, but you can't start a war over it, either. Tell you what; I'll ride out there in the morning and see if I can't get them to move."

Summer looked glum. "They won't," he said. "They're a bunch of slab-sided Texans—you know the kind, smile in your face with one hand on their guns."

"Yeah," the sheriff said as he rose. "Well, I'll talk to them in the morning, John. Good night."

"'Night."

He left the saloon, bought a bath, then went to the hotel and was starting up the stairs to his room when the night clerk called to him. "There were a couple of lawmen in here looking for you a few minutes ago, Sheriff."

"Lawmen?"

"Yes. Out-of-towners. They said they would wait for you at your office."

Nat stood without moving for a moment, then he swore under his breath, turned about, descended the stairs with angry tread and went back out into the night. The two men at the jail were strangers to him. One was tall and thin, the other was slightly under middle height, with muscle punched into a tight skin. Of the two, the latter was older, and when Nat entered he rose.

"You Sheriff Hendrick?"

"I am."

The burly man thrust out a hand. "I'm Sheriff Beeton from over Nevada way. This here is one of my deputies, Slim Eggers." Nat acknowledged both introductions, crossed to his desk and sank wearily down.

"Whereabouts in Nevada, Sheriff?" he asked.

"North-eastern Nevada—Cedar County."

"That's where they made that big gold strike last year, isn't it?"

"Yep."

"You're quite a ways from home."

"Yep," Becton said, sitting down again, "and before I'm through I might be a lot farther, too."

"Trouble?" Nat asked, mildly.

Beeton snorted. "Enough to last me a lifetime," he said. "We got lots of mining going on up in Cedar County, Sheriff. Lots of gold's being taken out of the ground."

10

"So I've heard."

"Yep. And that's where the trouble started. There's a band of renegades operating in the goldfields, you see, an' they rob the miners about as fast as the miners dig up the gold. I don't expect we'll ever know how much they've gotten away with, but we do know how much they've taken off the stages in daylight hold-ups. One million dollars' worth of coarse gold."

Nat's brows shot up. "That much?" he said.

Beeton nodded. "It's a heap of money, isn't it?"

Nat agreed. "A heap," he said. "Where does it all go, Sheriff?"

"That's the puzzler, Mr. Hendrick. What's sold by miners goes to the Denver mint. What's stole just plain disappears."

"I see. Is that why you're here in Gorman's Crossing? You think the stolen gold is coming here?"

"No, not exactly. Me and Slim is on our way to San Francisco to talk to the government mint folks down there. We've made it a practice to talk to every lawman on the way. We'll have to lie over here a day or two: Slim's damned horse hurt his leg about four miles north of town." Sheriff Beeton put a thick hand on the edge of Nat's desk and drummed with his fingers. "We always ask if anyone's been paying with raw gold in the towns we pass through."

Nat shook his head. "Not here," he said. "Not that I've heard of, anyway, and I'm pretty sure I'd have heard, Sheriff. There isn't enough raw gold in circulation in Northern Arizona so that it wouldn't cause talk if someone was passing it."

"I didn't expect much else," Beeton said, without visible disappointment.

"Have you reason to think the outlaws are heading

this way?"

"I got no idea where they're heading," Beeton replied. "Or even if they've left Nevada. There's one thing that keeps me from finding out, too. On our way south we haven't run across a single stranger payin' his way with raw gold. Not a cussed one."

Nat's tiredness was falling away. He looked steadily at the silent deputy. "It doesn't disappear," he said, and the deputy grinned but remained silent.

"They aren't cashing it in," Beeton said with a heavy scowl. "Whoever's doing their thinking is smart. If a stranger or two would start throwing raw gold around, either in Nevada or down here, I'd have something to sink my teeth into. It hasn't been happening, in Nevada or any place else that I can find. Strangers passing through have been paying in money. Only known miners been paying with gold, and I've ridden myself to a frazzle checking on them."

"How about a ring of miners turned outlaw?"

Beeton's scowl deepened. "Maybe yes," he said, "and maybe no. The idea's come to me, but so far I can't prove or disprove it. I can tell you one thing though; the same idea's occurred to a lot of Cedar County miners: there've already been a few killings over someone accusing someone else of being part of the ring."

"You must have *some* ideas," Nat said, watching Beeton's face.

"Yep, I got a few," the Nevadan conceded. "I think this is about the slickest band of outlaws that ever operated in the West, an' I think a mighty smart man is directing things. But I *don't* think the miners are mixed up in it. Nossir; these are experienced outlaws, men who've been robbing for a long time—they aren't miners."

12

"What are they doing with the gold?"

"I got to guess at that," Beeton said. "They can't just bury it, because they got to sell some for cash to live on. All right. They dassen't sell it in Nevada, down here in Arizona, or over in Idaho or Utah, because I've got flyers out to every blessed town in those places." Beeton's scowl lightened, his eyes narrowed. "I think they're getting it out of my territory some secret way; sell it either back East or down in San Francisco, have the cash brought back to Nevada, and divide it."

Nat nodded. His weariness was gone. "And where can they sell it?"

Beeton began wagging his head before Nat was finished speaking. "Mr. Hendrick," he said, "I been a lawman for twenty-five years. I've done every blessed thing that's going through your mind right now. I've got eleven special deputies. They've been checking every bank, every store, gambling house and assay office in Nevada. I've written to every sheriff in Idaho and Utah. I've had twenty-four-hour watches put on every bullion shipment leavin' Nevada Territory. I've had posses on the roads an' trails questioning and searching travellers from sun-up to sun-up. Do you know what I've learnt from all that? Nothing!"

Nat put both elbows on the desk and rested his chin on his fists. "These men have stolen several million dollars' worth of gold," he said thoughtfully.

"Right."

"And none of it's turned up anywhere—that you know of."

"Right again."

"But these outlaws are still operating in your county?"

"Right as rain."

"Well," Nat said, "they're cashing it in *somewhere*, Sheriff. They've got to; it doesn't make sense any other way. What's the advantage of stealing a million dollars if you can't use it?"

"There ain't any. It's got to be the way they dispose of it that'll lead us to 'em. If it takes me the rest of the year, I'm going to visit every mint in the United States, find out who they're buying raw gold from, then check back on every seller."

"That might take you longer than six months Nat said. "Especially if they're selling to the mints through more than one seller."

"Well," Beeton said resignedly, "I can't be any worse off than I am."

The sound of gunshots down the road interrupted Nat's thoughts. He rose without a word and moved swiftly towards the door. Outside, the town lay moon-limned and dark, except down by the saloon where a number of hip-shot horses stood. There, with orange light falling through the windows to lie softly in the roadway's layers of dust, men were passing out through the spindle-doors. He went forward, pushed past and entered the room. Smoke-haze, like gauze, limited visibility. Nat went toward the bar and caught the barman's eye. "Who fired those shots?" he asked.

Three travel-stained cowboys a few feet down the bar, standing beneath an old stuffed owl, wings spread as though seeking to fly through the murk, turned gently toward the sheriff. One of them, a lanky man with Texas sideburns, said, "I did."

"What's your name?"

"Willard Hays, Sheriff. Folks call me Will."

"There's a town ordinance against shooting inside the city limits, Hays."

14

"I didn't know that," the Texan said slowly. "We're new hereabouts."

"Where you from?"

"Idaho, Sheriff. We're just passin' through. We got a trail-herd north of town a piece."

"How long are you going to be around Gorman's Crossing?"

"Well, we figured to hang around long enough to rest up our critters and wash the dust away, Sheriff." The wide-set sun-paled eyes were unblinking. "Anyway, I didn't do no harm, Sheriff. Ask the barkeep."

"What did you shoot at?"

Hays moved his head backwards. "That there stuffed owl over the back bar. At his left eye, Sheriff."

Nat looked up. The owl, which had graced the back bar as long as he could remember, had a black hole where its left glass eye had been. "Any damages, Paul?" he asked the bartender.

"Naw, no harm done, Sheriff. Been going to throw that thing out for a long time, anyway."

To Hays Nat said, "Finish your drink, take your friends with you and go on back to camp. The next time you ride to town leave your guns behind."

"Sure," Hays said, staring steadily at the sheriff. "Sure enough; an' we'll be back, Sheriff. A feller gets powerful dry on these summer drives."

Nat considered the men for a moment. Then he asked if they knew of any other trail herd in the area where they were camped. Hays said he did not, but that a local herd was nearby, which was the answer Nat wanted. "Who's bossing your outfit, Hays?"

"Me."

"Is this your first drive?"

Hays smiled. "Lord, no, sheriff. I been makin' drives

15

since I was a button. From Canada to Mexico."

"Is that your business?"

"Yassir; buy cattle, make up a market an' sell 'em."

"Where are you bound for with this herd?"

"Mebbe Fort Apache, if the Army'll pay enough—if not, then somewhere else. Bought 'em in Idaho. Been on the trail quite a spell with 'em."

"Do you have a road-brand?"

"Well, I use a road-*mark*, Sheriff." When Nat said no more, Hays, still smiling, said, "I'll pay for the owl, an' after this we won't shoot up your town. Now how about havin' a drink with us, Sheriff?" Nat had one, then left the saloon and met Sheriff Beeton and his deputy outside. Beeton was wearing a twinkle in his eyes.

"Boys off the trail letting off steam," he said. "Where's the best place to bed down, Sheriff?"
isn't it?"

"Come on, I'll show you." He led them to the hotel, saw that they got a room, then went to his own quarters and went to bed.

Above him as he lay in the darkness, suffocating heat from the tin roof blanketed the room with a sticky atmosphere, and through the open window near his head came more noise than air. He listened for a while, then fell into an uneasy and restless slumber.

CHAPTER 2

THE FOLLOWING MORNING NAT WAS HAVING BREAKFAST at Betty Aldridge's café when Russ came in and dropped down. Betty asked if he would like a cup of coffee and got a wordless nod. The sheriff finished eating, pushed his plate back and began twisting up a cigarette. "Hot," he said. "Going to be hotter than it was yesterday."

"Yeah," Russ grunted without interest. When Betty put his cup down he gazed vacantly into the black liquid.

"Reckon we'll ride out to Summer's gathering ground this morning and talk to some trail-herders camped there," the sheriff said, through an exhaled cloud of smoke.

"All right." Russ drained the cup and got up. "I'm ready."

Nat got up more slowly. "You could fetch our horses over to the rack from the livery barn," he said, and after Russ was gone he raised troubled eyes to Betty. "He's worse," he said. "Listen, Betty, I don't like to ask this, but could you go down there and talk to Carrie Lee?"

"Sure, Nat. I'll go down now."

"I'll be beholden, Betty . . . You know, there's nothing worse than a lawman with his mind on something else. That's how they get killed—thinking of things miles away, when they shouldn't be."

After Nat left the café Betty locked the door, left her apron on the counter and went down the alleyway to the little house with the picket-fence around it. A young woman met her at the door. Her eyes were round and unhappiness lay tightly across her face. She said in a low voice, "Come in, Betty. The house is a mess."

Betty entered, found a chair and sat down. It wasn't the untidiness of the house that struck her, it was the aura of tenseness in it. Not without truth she said, "I wish I had a house like this. I love it, Carrie Lee."

"I hate it," the pregnant girl said. She was slim and dark-haired with sharp, responsive features, and once she had been gay and lively and quick-tempered. All

17

this Betty saw with profound pity. "I hate everything about it!" She dropped down on a sofa and stared at Betty. "Are you and Nat going to the Saturday-night dance?"

"I don't know; he hasn't asked me."

"Men!" Russ's wife said with a rush of bitterness, her lovely mouth drawn down at the corner. "I used to go to all the dances, and afterwards we'd ride home by first daylight and cook a big breakfast."

"You wouldn't want to go to *all* of the dances, Carrie Lee."

The girl put a hand across her stomach with the bitterness rising to her eyes and shining out. "Like this?" she said.

"Honey, that's the most wonderful thing that will ever happen to you."

"No, it isn't! I wish I was back home at the ranch. I hate this town!"

"You'll like it here. You really will. Right now there are a lot of things that are hard, Carrie Lee, but—"

"Never! I despise everything about Gorman's Crossing. I'll be an old hag with wrinkled skin before Russ can get us out of here. I have to sit here day in and day out—night in and night out . . . I even hate the sight of myself!" The small hand across her stomach convulsed into a fist. "This is is like being buried alive, Betty. I ought to leave; I ought to go back home—and I would, except I'm ashamed. Look at me!" She stared at Betty, great, soft eyes dark with bitterness, glazed with welling points of tears.

Betty crossed to her side and took one hand into her own two hands and held it. Carrie Lee went up against her. "I'm afraid," she said, in a choked whisper, her body trembling. "So—afraid, Betty."

18

There came to them a sound of horses outside, of bootsteps pounding up the walk. Betty put an arm around Carrie Lee, and murmured, "Nothing will happen, honey. I'll be here, and so will Russ and Nat." Men's voices sounded through the thin walls from out on the porch; there was a quick ring of spurs. Carrie Lee pulled back, patting at her hair.

"I'm a sight," she said, blinking away tears. "Russ has forgotten something." She got up and fled from the room. Betty was on her feet when Russ came past the door. He stopped, stared at her, then went past. Moments later he returned, and still without speaking, passed outside. Betty picked up some scattered linen and folded it idly, then she too went outside. Nat was in the act of mounting when he saw her on the porch. He hesitated, giving her a level glance across the saddle-seat, then he sprang up, flicked a hand at her and loped away through the dancing heat with Russ trailing after. Russ neither waved nor looked back. There was something in the shape of his back, in the way his head rolled with the horse's movement, that screamed out in silence. Where Gorman's Crossing ended, Nat looked back. Betty was still looking after them. He said something harsh under his breath and bent a narrowed glance on Russ.

"Last night one of these Texans tried to shoot up the saloon," he said. "It'll pay to keep both eyes peeled while we're out here."

"I will."

Nat's glance lingered. He slowed until Russ was riding stirrup with him. There was no need for conversation, and in fact he felt no desire to talk, the way the heat pressed down upon them and burnt against his slitted eyes, but he spoke anyway, casually, idly.

"I'm sort of curious about this trail herd, Russ. The boss says he's an old hand at trailing but he doesn't use a road-brand."

"What does he use? I thought every drive used road-brands. What's to keep outside cattle from getting into his herd?"

"Well, he said he uses a road-*mark*. That's what I'm curious about."

"Oh, an ear-mark or something like that," Russ said, and began to lapse back into his stony reverie.

"You're from Texas," Nat said. "Is that the way they do it down there?"

Russ's eyes cleared slowly and he shook his head. "No, not that I've ever heard of, anyway. Course, I only made a couple of drives. Up north they use road-marks; when I went up the trail to Montana Territory in '73 we ran into a number of marked herds on the trail. Some had dewlaps, some had wattles, and a couple had just plain earmarks." The deputy's face cleared as his mind went back to happier days. "I was told up there that some buyers won't take a herd with more than one brand on 'em, and that other buyers want the original bills of sale. Sometimes those things get lost, so the trail-herders use roadmarks instead of brands, then they write their own bills of sale for every road-marked critter and there's no trouble."

The land ahead lay still and drowsy under the pale yellow sun, and long before they got to the herd they smelled it. Closer still, they could hear the heat-muted call of riders who were out watching the grazing animals.

"There's a wagon," Russ said, arm out-flung Nat saw without speaking. Far to the west were cattle strung out grazing. Nearer, watching the animals, two riders were

20

squatting in the shade of their horses, smoking. As they rode nearer, the wagon stood out sharply. It was a battered old vehicle with dirty canvas stretched loosely over the bows. Riders' equipment was scattered around, and an emaciated looking older man wearing a flour-sack apron and a floppy-brimmed hat was peeling potatoes into a large kettle. He looked up as they approached, paring knife frozen in mid-air, then he got up and whistled. Almost at once two men came from the far side of the wagon. Nat recognized them both. One was Hays, the other was one of his companions of the night before. Hays walked forward a few feet and halted, wide-legged, thumbs hooked in his shell-belt.

"Howdy, Sheriff."

Nat returned the greeting as he swung down. After Russ was introduced Hays dredged up his slow and lazy smile. "Did the barkeep change his mind about damages to the owl?" he asked.

"No," Nat replied. "We just rode out to look at your herd and talk a little."

Hays waved toward the grazing animals. "He'p yourselves," he said. "That's all of them, out yonder."

"How many riders have you got?"

"Five, counting the cook—only I usually don't," Hays answered, his smile widening.

"All Texans?"

"Every man jack of 'em, Sheriff. Us Texas boys sort of hang together."

"Whereabouts in Idaho did you buy those cattle, Hays?"

"Around Fort Hall. 'Course they're from different owners. Must be thirty brands amongst 'em."

"What kind of a road-mark do you use?"

Hays turned slowly and pulled his hat forward against

21

the glare of the sun. He squinted toward the nearest animals a moment before he said, "A brisket dewlap. Look there; see that butt-headed cow yonder? See the dewlap on her?"

Nat and Russ saw: the cow had her head up, watching them. Hanging from her brisket was a dangling white appendage about ten inches long. The flesh had been sliced upwards, then permitted to hang down while it healed. The result was a long, white strip of hide which swung from side to side as the animal moved. It was an easily seen mark, and although neither Nat nor Russ had ever seen a dewlap quite so long before, both agreed it was a very effective mark of identification.

"Well," the nut-brown and stringy Texan said, "I learnt ye'rs back there's 'nough trouble trailin' cattle, 'thout having to stop an' cut back strays that join the herd along the way. With my mark, there, we can tell a stray as far as we can see, an' he's turned back before some irate local cowman comes bustin' up all lathered up and loaded for bear." Hays turned toward the wagon. "Come on over in the shade," he said, and when they were out of the sun he raised his voice: "Cookie! That coffee handy?"

"Yup; want some?"

"Yeah, three cups of it."

Hays began making a cigarette. When he was finished he held the sack out toward Nat and Russ. Both declined and Nat said, "Your cattle look good for being driven this late in the year."

Hays squatted down with his back to the wagon's nearwheel before replying. "We've had pretty fair feed so far," he said. "We trailed east along the Blackfoot River bottoms and took our time. Plenty green feed that way. When we hit the dry land we didn't try to make no

22

time, an' sweat off the lard. So far they've held up pretty well."

Nat said, "You had a visitor yesterday, didn't you?"

Hays' pouched-up eyes moved to the sheriff's face and stayed there. "Oh," he said after a moment. "I get it now. I understand why you're out here, Sheriff. Well, yes, we had a caller; big red-faced feller an' a couple of his riders. Feller named Summer; his brand's a pine-tree. Yeah. Well, we sort of come to an agreement. He's got his herd about a mile west."

"This is his gathering ground you're on."

Hays gazed at his cigarette. His face was a lean, tanned mask. "That's what he told me, Sheriff. Now you know this here land don't belong to no one—unless it's the Apaches hereabouts." The smile returned, but Hays' small eyes were mirthless. "Shucks, we're going to move on. All we want is a little rest. My herd won't hurt his graze very much."

"Maybe not," Nat said, "but you'd make it a lot easier on all of us if you'd move east a few miles. That's open country too, and no one'd care if you camped there a month."

The cook brought three cups of coffee, set them down on the ground without a word and withdrew. Hays smoked and sipped coffee and seemed to be considering his answer. Russ took off his hat and felt the coolness of drying sweat on his head. He noticed that Nat's face was blanked over and expressionless, and that the sheriff was gazing steadily out where the cowboys were keeping a close vigil over the cattle. Then Hays spoke again, his drawl more pronounced, his words slow-paced.

"I could move, I reckon, but you know, Sheriff, this don't impress me as a real friendly country. Now you

23

take last night, f'instance. You sort of run me out of town. Now here you are again, wanting me to move my herd." The sun-faded eyes were open wide enough for Nat to see the devil-points of fire in their depths: this was a dangerous man, a soft-speaking, insincere-smiling, deadly-as-a-rattlesnake Texan.

"Last night you broke a town ordinance," he said, "and today all I'm asking is that you move far enough east so that Pine Tree can finish their round-up the way they always have, and on the ground they've always used."

"What about water?"

"There's the river two miles east."

Hays nodded as though the information pleased him.

"And Injuns?" he asked.

"Well, there are always Indians somewhere around," Nat said. "But most of them stay on the reservation."

Hays smiled again. "Most of 'em, Sheriff?"

"You're no greenhorn, Hays. You know how Apaches are. The young bucks get restless for a little raiding now and then."

"Not on my herd they don't," Hays said. "You got any notion they might be east a ways? I mean, you wouldn't send me over there hopin' they'd lift my topknot and make off with my critters, would you?"

Nat looked squarely at the Texan, then he said, "I think you know better than that, Hays. I don't think you're that poor a judge of men."

Something in the sheriff's tone calmed the Texan a little. "Now, Sheriff, I was just makin' talk, you know that." He got up and flexed his legs. "All right, I'll move. Not before tomorrow, though."

Nat and Russ also stood up. "Much obliged," the sheriff said, starting toward his horse.

24

"Any time at all, Sheriff," Hays said, watching them go with his smile tight drawn. "See you in town some time—without my gun, of course."

Nat and Russ rode back through the pulsing heat, their mounts making slow and uncomfortable progress as far as the first shade. There, while they rested the animals, Russ said, "That's quite a road-mark, Nat. It's three inches longer than it has to be."

"Sure is. Well, let's get back to town."

They were nearing the outskirts when Russ looked over and said, "What's bothering you, Nat?"

"I wish it was just one thing," the sheriff replied. "Right now I'm thinking about Hays. He said he'd trailed his herd east along the Blackfoot River, didn't he?"

"Yes. What's wrong about that?"

"The Blackfoot River runs north and south."

Russ said no more until they had left their animals at the livery barn and were crossing toward the office. Then he said, "Are you sure about that?"

"Pretty sure. I've picked up a few prisoners at Fort Hall, in Idaho. That river doesn't run east, but just to make sure we'll ask around."

"Hays could have been mistaken."

"I hope he was," Nat said, holding the door open until the deputy had passed through, then closing it against the yellow glare. "But it seems to me if I'd trailed cattle along a river I'd know which way it ran."

Russ's forehead drew low over his eyes. He watched Nat hang up his hat, wipe sweat off his face with a limp handkerchief, and sit down behind the desk.

"Rustled cattle, Nat?"

"I doubt that. You know, Russ, it's pretty hard to hang a rustler unless the cattle he's stolen have been re-

25

branded when they're in his possession. A trail-driver as smart as Hays wouldn't stick his neck into a noose by road-marking animals that didn't belong to him."

"Then he just has his directions crossed up."

"Like I said, I hope that's all there is to it. It's too hot out to be riding around the country these days."

"Yeah. Well, is there anything you want me to do, in particular?"

Nat looked hard at the desk-top. "Russ. . . No, I guess not. Go on home if you want to."

"Thought I'd go down to the saloon for a while."

Nat watched his deputy leave the office. "You do that," he said to the emptiness around him. "Get damned good and drunk; that ought to simplify a lot of things for you. Yeah, you do that, kid."

He filed a number of wanted-flyers and then went in search of the raffish old man who served as night jailer. Finding him never posed much of a problem; he was usually among the spit-and-whittle fraternity of oldsters who had a bench on the shady side of the livery barn, where they spun improbable tales of their youth. The old man was there, smelling faintly of whisky. He got up when Nat approached, and smiled uncomfortably.

"Howdy, Sheriff."

"Howdy, Sheepy. You fed the prisoner today?"

"Now y'know, I was just fixin' t'go over and do that."

"Yeah, sure you were. Someday you're going to forget 'em and one'll bite your arm off."

"Has Miz' Betty got the grub ready, you reckon?"

Nat fixed the old man with a stern look. "Have you ever known her not to, Sheepy?"

"Well, no."

"Then go on."

26

Walk with me a piece," the old man said, and as they crossed the road he lowered his voice to a conspiratorial whisper. "Injuns're out again, Nat. Heard a feller who'd just ridden in from over by Duncan tell Old Man Smith."

"What did he say?"

"A bunch of bronco Chiricahuas jumped the reservation couple of days back and took to the hills."

"Heading this way?"

"He didn't say."

"All right, Sheepy. Go feed our horse-thief."

The old man craned his neck and squinted his eyes. "Ain't you going to do anything, Nat?"

The sheriff stepped up onto the plankwalk and halted. "What can I do? I'm not going Indian hunting in weather like this unless I know where they are, and that they've done something illegal."

"Injuns never do anything that ain't illegal."

"Maybe. Sheepy, you've been on Indian hunts. Did you ever find them when they didn't want to be found?"

"Not very cussed many," the jailer conceded gruffly.

"Then let's just wait. Maybe they'll go south toward Mexico."

Sheepy turned away heading down the plankwalk toward Betty Aldridge's café He stumped along grumbling to himself, and Nat, watching him, shook his head, paused a moment before heading for the saloon, and looked up and down the road.

The first shadows of late afternoon were coming out, tentative fingers of shade that grew and widened. A high-wheeled freighter passed, grinding deep into the dusty roadway with its burden, boring northward at a snail's pace. Over in front of the bank George Semple was in earnest conversation with Ulen Fritz who owned the mighty Maltese Cross Cattle Company. Somewhere southward a tinny piano sent wavering echoes of *Lorena* through the dying day, and behind Smith's livery barn an anvil, clear as a bell, made truer music. Nat let the sounds go into him, and because he was in the overhang's shade, he felt at peace and in no haste to move. A voice spoke his name softly and he turned. It was Sheriff Beeton and his silent deputy.

"Howdy. Been out ridin' today?"

Nat nodded. "Had to talk some Texan trail-herders into moving their cattle off local ground."

"Pretty cussed hot," Beeton said.

"Yeah. How's Mr. Eggers' horse today?"

"Still pretty gimpy, Sheriff," Beeton replied. "I guess we'll be held up another day or two." His shiny face brightened. "Buy you a drink?"

"All right."

They walked south together, with Deputy Eggers behind, a tall, wasted-looking man content to linger in the shadows of other men. At the saloon Nat looked around for Russ. He wasn't in the room. Beeton asked Nat's pleasure, and when the beer came he said, "Let's take it to a table, my cussed feet swell in this kind of weather." When they were seated Beeton thrust out his short, thick legs and sighed. "Never did care for summer," he said. "If the waterholes don't dry up, then the feed does. Take winter any time." He looked about the half-empty room. "Me and Slim was saying that you sure keep an orderly town here, Sheriff."

"It's quiet most of the time," Nat replied. "Tell me something, Beeton. Have you ever been around Fort Hall over in Idaho?"

"Lots of times, why?"

"Which way does the Blackfoot River flow?"

28

"It makes a bend near the mountains, then runs about north and south. Maybe a little north-west by south. You got a bet on which way it flows?"

"No," Nat said. "I just wanted to make sure I remembered right. A man'd have a hard time trailing cattle east along it, wouldn't he?"

Beeton smiled wryly. "It'd be a little hard to do," he said. "He'd have to turn the river plumb around. Slim, how about fetching us three more beers from the bar?"

"Sure."

When the deputy was gone Beeton's drowsy eyes fixed themselves on Nat's face. "Thought any more about my outlaws?"

"A little," Nat said.

"What'd you come up with?"

"A belief that you'll never catch them by trying to back-track mint purchases of gold."

"How then?"

"By figuring how that gold leaves Cedar County and catching the men who move it."

Slim returned, put the glasses down and swung a leg over his chair. Beeton drank deeply for a moment and wiped his mouth with the back of a hairy hand. "I'll say it again, Sheriff," Beeton replied wearily. "I've had every bullion shipment traced; I've had every traveler searched; I've had every . . ."

"But they're still getting it out, aren't they?"

"Yes."

"Then it's pretty clear you're missing something, Beeton."

The conversation went no further. John Summer entered the saloon with a day's growth of gray-glinting beard on his face, his cheek-bones chalked with alkali dust, and dry-sweat stains across his forehead. He stood briefly in the doorway, reached up and pushed his hat back, and his hairline shown startling white where the hat had been. "Ahhh, Nat," he said, widening his glare-tightened eyes. The sheriff left Beeton and Eggers and went to the bar with Summer, who thumped a big fist for beer then turned hip-shot toward the lawman. "You got 'em to move, didn't you?"

"I talked to them about it."

Summer drained the glass of beer and ground it down hard upon the counter, calling for a refill. "Well, they moved, Nat. Commenced moving early this afternoon. Now they're camped about a half mile from the river."

"They told me they wouldn't move until tomorrow."

Summer shrugged, drank the second beer and shoved the glass away. "They did it this afternoon. I sat my horse on a hill watching them."

"All right," Nat said, seeing the tumult in Summer's eyes. "What's wrong with that?"

"Nothing. Not a damned thing." Summer pushed his long lips together and regarded the sheriff with intent eyes.

"Where's your deputy?"

"Why, home, I expect."

"No, he ain't, Nat."

Something tightened around Nat's heart. Summer removed his hat, swiped at his forehead with a shirt-sleeved arm and replaced the hat. "You recollect that Duncan mercantile robbery a couple days back?"

"I heard about it, yes."

"There were two outlaws held up the store, robbed the safe and got away with eighty-five hundred dollars."

"That's right."

"Then they rode off and nobody knew where they

went."

"Listen, John . . ."

"Your deputy knew, Nat."

"*What!*"

"He must've known. I was sitting up there on a hill watching those Texans move their herd, and directly I saw a rider north of me, farther back in the hills. He was riding hell for leather. I circled around into some trees and watched him. He wasn't one of my Pine Tree riders and he wasn't one of them Texans. Pretty soon another rider came a-helling out of the trees chasing the first man. The shadows were fallin', Nat, and it was impossible for me to identify either one of 'em, but I could tell from the way they were ridin' that one was after the other one. The one who was behind started shooting, and directly the first rider's horse went down. I tied my horse, took my carbine, and crept up as close as I dared. The second rider came chargin' up, flung off and ran toward the first man . . .Without a word he threw up his carbine and shot him . . ."

Summer's intent stare grew still. "It was Russ done the killing, Nat."

"Who was the other one?"

Summer's reply was delayed. Finally he said, "I went back, got on my horse and rode out where Russ was standin'. When he saw me he said the dead man was one of the Duncan robbers."

"Well . . .?"

"Nat," Summer said in a quiet way, "there was two things about that killing. One, Russ never gave the other feller a chance to surrender. Two, the man Russ killed *wasn't armed!*"

31

CHAPTER 3

SUNLIGHT BURNED AGAINST THE EARTH, CATCHING THE thin and bitter flashes of mica in the roadway's dust and throwing them upwards into the yellow glare. Heat hung over Gorman's Crossing layer upon layer until it became a solid substance that men had to lean into; it shimmered suddenly and in some inexplicable way thinned the air so that men had to suck hard to fill their lungs. The road was deserted; the few horses at the racks hung their heads listlessly.

Nat leaned upon the wall over by the window, and Russ stood near the desk. Betty had spent the night with Carrie Lee, and Doctor Simpson had delivered the baby. A sick-soft feeling was in Nat; a sense of failure; a feeling that the words behind his lips had no meaning. He watched an ostler across the way sprinkling water down the livery barn's main alley.

"Say it," Russ said finally, flat-toned and sharp-speaking.

Nat didn't look around. "I never wanted to say anything less in my life, Russ."

"Say it anyway," the deputy said from a depth of bitterness. "I killed him for the reward, and you don't want a deputy who'd do a thing like that."

Russ left the window, went to the desk and sank down. "That wasn't what I was going to say."

"No?" Two sunken eyes went to Nat's bowed head and stayed there.

"No. You went riding after you left the saloon yesterday afternoon, and somehow you came onto those men back in the hills." Nat's head raised up. "What were you riding back there for—so far from Carrie Lee,

Russ?"

"I had no idea the baby was coming, Nat. Honest to God I didn't. She told me once it wasn't due until September. Listen, if I'd known—even the way she feels toward me—I'd have been there; I'd have been there if all the outlaws in Arizona were . . ."

"All right, you've got a son."

"Nat . . ."

"Let me finish. You didn't know about the baby. You didn't want to go home yesterday afternoon, so you rode out into the hills. You came onto those two men."

"And one of them took a shot at me. The other one jumped onto a saddled horse and ran. I ran after him . . . I shot him."

"Russ, he wasn't armed. I rode to their camp this morning before sun up with the Pine Tree outfit. We saw how the other one had escaped, leaving everything behind. All the things belonging to the man you killed were lying there—his six-gun and his carbine."

"I . . . Nat, when his horse went down he jumped up, facing me. I . . . didn't look, Nat, I just fired. Listen, I had no idea who he was until I found that wanted-flyer in his shirt-pocket."

"Russ, no man shoots an unarmed person."

"I *told* you—I didn't know he was unarmed!"

"But he was standing there, probably waiting to surrender, or he'd have run for cover, and you killed him."

Russ's cheek twitched; he turned aside to hide it from the sheriff. His eyes stung and a lowering great weight thrust against the slump of his shoulders.

". . . people usually believe the worst about lawmen, Russ. Things they can interpret into murder, like this killing, hurts all lawmen."

33

"I don't need a ⟨ ⟩dam sermon," Russ said wildly, flinging around. "I get enough of those at home! Just take this badge and shut up!"

Nat rose and stood erect behind the desk. "'That's exactly what I'm *not* going to do. You're going to wear that badge and you're going to live this down."

"I won't! We'll get out of here. Gorman's Cross—"

"You'll wear it, and every time it burns your hand, Russ, you'll remember what you did. You aren't going to get out of this just by throwing that badge on the desk, not by a damned sight."

"Carrie Lee's always hated this town."

"Sure she has, and that's another thing—but let me tell you this, Russ: you aren't going to run out an' leave me to face the talk alone."

"You? You didn't have anything to do with it."

"I hired you, didn't I? I had the circuit judge swear you in, didn't I? I've been telling folks what a top-notch deputy you've been, haven't I? You think I'm going to sit here and take the abuse alone? Not on your life. Now you put that badge back on and you go home and sit with Carrie Lee. Betty's got her café to run, she can't be spending *all* her time down there."

Russ made no move toward the badge. Nat waited, then his voice got sharp-toned and whip-like, and he pointed downward. "*Take it!* That's better. Now put it on. Fine. Now go home . . . Walk down that plankwalk like you owned it. Go on."

Moments after his deputy had departed Nat went to the door, opened it and stood in the opening gazing northward. Russ went past the idlers as though he did not see them. Nat's glance hardened when he saw how men turned away. His grip on the edge of the door made the knuckles stand out white-sharp and hurting.

34

Sunlight poured out of the low west, the color of fire. Riders drifted past the sheriff's office and a few looked over and nodded. Big Ulen Fritz came down the plankwalk with his boots making hushed thunder. He stopped near Nat, his head facing northward, his pale eyes on the diminishing back of Russ Bell. He let go a long, deep sigh. "Damn fool kid," he said. "Does he have any idea how long it'll take him to live that down?"

"Not yet he hasn't."

"No, I expect not." The big head turned. "You know what folks're saying, Nat?"

"I can guess."

"Get rid of him."

"I've got two years of my term left, Ulen . . ."

"Unless they impeach you, Nat."

A shrug.

Fritz scowled; it made his broad, red face look fierce. "He's having other troubles, too, isn't he?"

"Some," Nat admitted.

Fritz looked down where Russ no longer was. "I remember when I owed Semple a little money," he said reflectively. "He told everyone in town about it . . . How about Carrie Lee, Nat?"

"What about her?"

"Folks say they don't get along, that she wants to leave him."

"Folks talk too much. How long've you been married, Ulen?"

". . . Yeah, I know." The pale eyes hardened. "Suppose I buy that note from Semple and keep it until the kid can repay it."

"I would, if I could," Nat replied.

"All right, I'll get it . . . Nat?"

35

"Yes."

"Are you thinking of what'll happen if you fire him?"

"Partly that, Ulen. He gets five hundred dollars for that outlaw. If I turn him out he's going to start thinking about tracking other outlaws down for the bounty. And it's partly something else; Betty says he loves Carrie Lee and that she loves him."

"And now their baby."

"Yeah. How was it the first year your oldest boy was married, Ulen?"

"Well, he had his mother and me—and Bedelia's folks. He didn't have to face the whole world single-handed." Fritz shifted his feet. "I'll see you, Nat," he said, and started across the roadway toward the bank.

Nat went back into the office and closed the door. Later, when Sheepy came in, he was lying stretched out full length on the old leather sofa, watching the fading color of the sky through the window. The old man said, "Are you sick, Sheriff?"

Nat got up, ran bent fingers through his hair and put his hat on. "No, I'm not sick, dammit. Can't a man rest his bones without someone thinking he's sick?"

Sheepy looked startled. He moved quickly toward the cell-block door, poked his head out and said, "Russ didn't really kill that outlaw in cold blood, did he?"

"He killed an outlaw," the sheriff said bleakly. "That's all anyone has to know." He went to the door, passed through and slammed it hard. Sheepy pursed his lips, scowled, then went angrily out of sight.

Betty was at the café when Nat got there. She saw the pain in his face and thought once again, a thought she'd often had: that men on the frontier were meant to be a part of dust and struggle, to know harshness and to get pleasure from the little intervals between. Without

36

speaking she put a piece of pie in front of him, drew off two cups of coffee, and leaned against the pie-table while drinking hers.

"How is she?" he asked, finally.

"She'll be all right. Russ came home just before I left."

"Yeah. You make this pie? It's good."

"Tell me about the killing, Nat. Did it happen the way people say?"

"I don't know what people say, Betty, but I know only two men saw it. One was Russ, the other was John Summer. Outside of me, I don't think Russ's told anyone. You know John. Something like this'll lie inside him till Doomsday."

"You rode up there this morning."

"So I did."

"Well . . ."

"What's the difference? Give me another piece of pie, will you?"

"Then it's true. He shot that man without giving him a chance."

"He didn't know the damned fool was unarmed. He was riding like an Indian, chasing him. The feller's horse got shot, and he jumped up facing Russ. He shot . . . The feller had no gun on him. Betty, those things happen. Russ was excited; someone'd taken a shot at him earlier." Nat looked down at the pie she set in front of him, then back up to her face. "Does Carrie Lee know?"

Betty shook her head and poured them both another cup of coffee. "Well," she said, "eat it, you wanted it."

"I'm not really hungry," Nat said, pushing the plate back.

"Carrie Lee'll hear about it soon enough, Nat.

37

Everyone who's been in here today was talking about it. What will the Town Council say?"

"They'll ask me to fire him and I'll tell them to go to hell."

"And they'll fire *both* of you."

"That's all right, Betty. I'm a pretty good blacksmith. I used to make more by accident as a blacksmith than I make now as a sheriff on purpose."

"What about the other one—the one that got away?"

"Russ and I're going after him in the morning. He can't get very far." Nat put both elbows on the counter and rested his head on his hands. "If he's lucky, we'll catch him. If he's unlucky the Apaches'll get him."

"Are they out again?" Betty asked, a shadow passing across her face. Nat nodded. "Then take a big posse with you, Nat."

He smiled. "You think I could get a posse to ride with me when I'm taking Russ along? Not now, Betty."

"Then leave him and take the posse."

"Uh-huh. There's enough bad feeling around town for someone to try and bait him into a gunfight. I don't want to come back tomorrow night and have to bury Russ and tell Carrie Lee she's a widow an' her two-day-old son's an orphan." He looked at the wall-clock and got up. "I'll be back in a little while, and maybe we could go for a walk in the moonlight."

"All right," she said, and watched him leave.

Two hundred feet south of the café Nat ran into George Semple. What the banker had in mind was etched across his face. Nat saw it and gave him no chance to say it. "Mr. Semple, I'm not going to fire Russ. Tomorrow we're both going after the outlaw that escaped. If you're dead-set on replacing him, then you'll have all day to find replacements for both of us. Good night." He pushed past and disappeared into the doorless opening of the hotel.

Semple remained rooted. His face swelled with angry dark blood, and his mouth snapped closed. When Sheriff Beeton and Deputy Eggers passed him, he did not see them.

Nat was at the desk getting his key when Beeton approached. "You know," the Nevadan said casually, "I did that once, when I was his age, Sheriff. Funny thing; folks in Cedar County wouldn't take on about it like they're doin' here. A dead outlaw's just one less to sweat about."

"I guess folks in Gorman's Crossing don't have much else to take on about," Nat said, moving around Beeton toward the stairs. "If you're in the saloon later tonight I'll buy you a drink."

"We'll be there," Beeton said, watching Nat go up the stairs. Then he turned to his deputy. "Slim, there goes the kind of a lawman I wish I was. His mind's workin' all the time."

The heat in Nat's room was stifling. He began to change his clothes over by the window. It was no cooler there but he had a good view of the road. Several riders loped past and a number of men were talking in front of the livery barn. He guessed the context of their conversation with no effort. Somewhere north of the hotel a dog-fight was in progress; sounds of animal fury knifed through the thick atmosphere with unusual clarity. He poked his head out and looked north. The animals were fighting in the dust before Russ Bell's house. As he watched, the deputy came flinging angrily down the walk, grabbed both combatants by the scruff of their necks and flung them apart. None of the gathering spectators offered to help. When Russ started

39

back toward his house they watched him pass in stony silence. From the porch Russ looked back. The men had not moved; they were watching him. He turned abruptly and disappeared inside.

Russ had contrived a rope-operated fan above Carrie Lee's bed. He took his place in a darkening corner and worked the ropes gently.

His wife lay motionless, dark hair loose around the drawn paleness of her cheeks. She would not look at Russ, and that was what stabbed deep like the point of a sharp knife. She hadn't spoken to him since he'd returned from Nat's office. Even when he had been rigging up the fan, and before that, when he had taken the chair beside her bed.

The baby was in a rickety cradle. From where he stood Russ could trace out the wizened red face, could see how frail and plain the baby was.

Doctor Simpson arrived with his unhurried, confident bearing. He cast a long look at Russ, a briefer one at Carrie Lee, and bent over the cradle with his whiskers jutting outward like splayed fingers. His stethoscope looked enormous against the baby's chest, then it lifted and Simpson moved toward the bed. Carrie Lee spoke in a washed-out way. "He sleeps all the time. He's sick, isn't he?"

Simpson removed the stethoscope. His eyes kept watching her face, very sharp, very humane eyes. "There isn't a thing in the world wrong with him, Carrie Lee. He's been through quite an ordeal, you know. Just wait—give him a week or two; you'll wish he'd sleep."

Russ noticed how his wife looked steadily at the doctor, saw the heavy anguish and resentment in her eyes and knew Simpson saw it too. He started forward. The doctor shifted his stance the smallest bit and blocked his advance, then, as though he had not cut off the view of her husband, he said to Carrie Lee: "He's a fine boy—a fine boy. He has his mother's beautiful eyes and his father's great patience. I don't think anyone could ask for more, Carrie Lee." They both saw her lips grow straight and tight for a moment. Simpson remained cheerful in the face of her settled and resenting manner. He pocketed the stethoscope and stood lost in thought for a moment. Then he looked at the mother again, and over at Russ. He seemed to be listening to the silence in the room, estimating its depth and meaning. He cleared his throat. "Carrie Lee, your husband killed a man last night," he said. "Now I want you to know something. That man deserved killing." That was all he said, and the closeness of the room descended again.

Carrie Lee lay with her head turned, watching the doctor. When he started for the door he brushed Russ's arm with his fingers. They left together. In the parlor Russ turned around. "Why did you tell her that? She hates me enough without *that*."

"Russ, I can't pretend very well. I know how she's been feeling lately. I also want you to understand something; this is the time when you can expect no reasonableness from her; it's a time when her thoughts are turned inward, and as long as she's feeling sorry for herself she'll feed that self-pity with whatever is handy. In this case it's resentment of you, son. I wanted to jar her away from that. I wanted to shock her into thinking of you in a different way—even as a killer—any way but as the cause of her pain and suffering. I avoided the details of the killing on purpose. I told her that outlaw deserved to die. I want her to think about that, to imagine all sorts of reasons why you were a hero."

41

Simpson took up his hat from a chair and moved toward the front door. With his hand on the latch he said, "What I said about patience I meant, Russ, and you're going to need it, lots of it. She'll come around, boy, she'll understand; just give her lots of time."

"No, she won't," Russ blurted, and Simpson was shocked to see that he was caving in, that tears were being squeezed from around his tightly closed eyes. He stepped away from the door, struck Russ on the back and shook him.

"You're not the first man who's done that, either, Russ." Simpson's hand dropped to the deputy's arm and pulled. "Come along with me," he said. "You need a stiff drink." He took Russ out into the black night, down the walk and toward the saloon. Two shadows, one tall and lean, the other short and massive, loomed up. It was Beeton and Eggers. Russ saw Beeton's blurred face bending toward him curiously.

"Anything wrong?" the Nevadan asked.

Russ stiffened against Beeton's stare and rapped his answer out short and sharp. "No!" he said, and moved past with Doctor Simpson.

At the café doorway Doctor Simpson poked his head in and called. When Betty appeared, in a fresh cotton dress, her taffy-colored hair piled high and cool-looking, he asked her to go sit with Carrie Lee for a while. She agreed with a silent nod, looking over Simpson's shoulder at the pale, glistening face of Russ Bell.

When they got to the saloon Russ hung back. Simpson's strong hand drew him on through the doors and into the tangy, stale air and the pale, hot light. Noise swept over them. The doctor found a wall table, pushed Russ into a chair and flagged for drinks. They were sitting there apart, yet a part of the revelry around them, when Nat Hendrick came through the doors, hesitated in the opening when he saw them, and worked his way through the crowd and drew a chair up to their table. "Have a drink," Simpson said, pushing the bottle and his own glass toward the sheriff. Nat drank and looked long at the doctor. Simpson shrugged with meaning and poured Russ another glassful. Someone brushed past and Nat looked around. It was Beeton and Eggers. They went to a far table occupied by an unconscious Maltese Cross rider and sat down. Neither ordered drinks. Beeton's eyes seemed drowsy, but from behind their heavy lids a shrewd and calculating look fanned out over the room. After a time he spoke to Slim Eggers.

"Mebbe it's good medicine to bring him here," he said in a drawl, "but it sure isn't very good sense. Look yonder at the bar."

Eggers looked. Two weaving Pine Tree riders were staring stonily at Russ Bell's back. One of them spoke and the second one went out into the crowd. Moments later there was a noticeable diminishing of sound in the room. Other cowboys were joining the group. Finally the bartender sensed something and looked in a worried way from the table where Nat, Russ, and Simpson sat, back to the low-talking rangemen. He seemed undecided as to what course to take, so he took none.

Eggers said "Yeah," very softly, and the word carried, something it would not have done minutes earlier. "Guess you're right."

More absorbed with his private thoughts, Nat was slower to sense the room's change. It was Doctor Simpson who looked up suddenly. When Nat heard his breath rush out he turned. Three men were behind his chair, their eyes widened in a fixed and ruthless way

43

upon Russ Bell. When he started to get up one of the cowboys put a hand on his shoulder and pushed, hard. "Set still, Sheriff. Just set still-like. Hey, Deputy, get up!"

Russ looked into their faces. Beyond them he saw four more faintly smiling but mirthless faces over by the bar. The crowd was fading along the wall.

"*Get up!*"

From over by the card-room door Joab Smith, whom everyone called Old Man Smith, struggled upwards from his table. "Here, you fellers," he said thickly. "That's the sheriff there. You better—"

"Shut up, old-timer," a loose-standing cowboy said from the bar. "Don't go buyin' yourself a hurt."

Old Man Smith's eyes cleared gradually. His mouth drew closed and his face paled. He sat back down.

"Hey, Deputy, you hard of hearin'? Them boys told you to get up."

Russ twisted farther around, looked at the men by the bar and gathered his legs under him. In one swift breath Nat said, "Don't do it!"

"What's the matter, Sheriff? 'Fraid if'n he has to face an *armed* man standin' up, he might get cut down?"

Nat twisted away from the hand on his shoulder, started to rise. A gun-barrel, cold and still, bored into the base of his skull. "Sit down, Sheriff!"

"Look at th' law," a slurred voice jeered. "Look at 'im settle down there easy-like and do-cile." A thin laugh rattled through the room. "It's different when they can't plug unarmed men, ain't it? Come on, Deputy, do like the feller told you—get up. Let's see what you got to say f'yourself about killin' that unarmed feller. Let's see what a murderer's got to say f'hisself."

Russ was moving when a booming voice burst into

44

the stillness. "Hold it! You there behind the sheriff—you drop that gun. *Drop it!* I'd just as soon blow you in two from behind as in front."

The cowboy holding his pistol against Nat's head grew stiff and tense. Into the hush came the sharp snippet of sound he knew to be the cocking of a handgun. His gun drew away and it wavered in his fist.

"For the last time—*drop it!*"

The gun fell.

"You other fellers there—move away from the bar. That's it—keep them hands wide, *real wide, damn you!*"

Nat twisted his head slowly. Beeton and Eggers were against the far wall, guns low and steady. He cast a quick look at his deputy. Russ was rising. Only Doctor Simpson hadn't moved; his face was gray.

"Looks like we got a jailful of real curly wolves," Beeton said to Nat in a voice edged with ice. "Real hell-roarers."

"Get their guns," Nat said to Russ, rage and humiliation burning in him. "You there," he said to the man who had held the six-gun to his head. "Who do you work for?"

"Pine Tree."

"What's your name?"

"Jack Quinn."

"You lead off behind Mr. Eggers here. The rest of you follow along to the jailhouse." When the sobered, silent cowboys were leaving the saloon under four guns, Doctor Simpson got up awkwardly from the table. A little color had returned to his face.

"Nat , I think I'll ride out to Pine Tree."

"Thanks, Doc. I'd appreciate that. John will want to know where they are, I expect."

45

At the sheriff's office each prisoner was frisked, his pockets emptied, and his name entered in a ledger. Russ locked them up. Beeton sprawled on the leather sofa and made a cigarette. Over his fingers he said, "Never saw such a hangdog-looking bunch of hell-roarers before. They sure lost their starch between the saloon an' here." He licked the paper, folded it over, popped the cigarette into his mouth and lit it. He was breaking the match when the door blew open and Doctor Simpson came in, one step ahead of big John Summer.

"Doc told me about what happened," the cowman said. "By golly, Nat, I wouldn't blame you if you'd lynched 'em. Where are they? Let me talk to 'em for a minute. I got some paying-off to do."

Russ Bell spoke from the cell-block doorway. "That won't change anything, Mr. Summer."

"Won't it! You listen to me, boy—"

"I learnt something today," Russ said. "Having to live with something is worse punishment than getting paid off so you can ride off and forget it."

Summer's eyes lingered with close intensity on the deputy's face. He closed his mouth and only the large, swelling pulse in the side of his neck showed that indignation still coursed rampant through him. It was Doctor Simpson who spoke next, in a quietly agreeing manner.

"John, some folks live and learn, and some just live. Why don't you let Nat keep them locked up a day or two before you make up your mind?"

Beeton pushed heavily up off the sofa. "You folks down here may not be as tough as the miners around Cedar County," he said, "but you got more sense. Well, me'n Slim got to get some sleep if we're goin' riding in the morning." He shambled across the room as far as

46

Nat's desk, then stopped with a squinty look. "We are goin' riding, aren't we, Sheriff?"

"I don't know what you're talking about."

"Well, me'n Slim been studying you out," Beeton said, "and we've concluded that you aim to go hunting for that other outlaw tomorrow. Now, since we got nothing to do, we figured you'd maybe rustle up a horse for Slim, and we'd sort of trail along."

Nat ran a hand over the scratchy edge of his jaw and regarded Sheriff Beeton wryly. "I'd be proud to have you along," he said. "You and Mr. Eggers."

Beeton went around John Summer, trailed by his deputy, and left the office. Doctor Simpson followed shortly after, and John Summer exhaled a mighty sigh and stood there wagging his head. "I can't understand why they'd do that, Nat. They were up there this morning—they saw the sign—they know how it happened."

"Everybody's a little bit against the law, John. John Barleycorn was mostly responsible tonight."

"Well," Summer said, looking over where Russ was tagging the shell belts of his Pine Tree riders and hanging them up, "I want you an' Russ to know right now that no Pine Tree rider draws a gun on lawmen and still works for me. No, Russ, I'm not mad any more. That's not it. There are some things I hold to be inexcusable, and throwing down on the law is one of 'em. Maybe they didn't mean it like that; I'm not sayin' they did—but nothing's changed. No man works for Pine Tree who draws on a sheriff. If I had a son and he did that, I'd fire him just as quick as any other rider."

Nat said, "Think it over, John. Think about it like Russ said. Riding away from Gorman's Crossing after throwing down on the law here will make it easier for them to forget it—or remember how easy it was and do it again. If they have to stay on and ride in here every few days and see Russ and me—it'll make them feel pretty cheap for a long time."

"Well, we'll see." Summer grew thoughtful. "You really going after that other one tomorrow, Nat?"

"Yes. He can't have gone far."

"I reckon not," Summer said in a dry tone. "By now the Injuns'll probably be making mincemeat out of him. You'd best take a big posse with you. There's no telling where those damned redskins are, in those mountains, but there's one thing sure: they'll see you long before you see them."

"I think four of us will be plenty," Nat said. "Well, John, I've got to get some sleep. See you when we get back."

"Yeah. *If* you get back."

CHAPTER 4

THERE WAS A STILLNESS TO THE DAWN WHEN THEY rode out of Gorman's Crossing the next day. A scent of scorched earth rose around them. Slim Eggers rode beside Russ, both steeped in silence, while up ahead Nat rode beside the Sheriff from Cedar County. "You know the country," Beeton said. "Where do you reckon he'll be?"

Nat lifted an arm, pointing north-west where the mountains' flanks came down upon the plain in dark outline. "If he knows the country, I think he'll be between Grave Creek near the bottom, and Apache Springs near that highest peak yonder. If he's a stranger," Nat dropped his arm and shrugged, "we'll

48

only find him by tracking."

Beeton studied the foothills as they got closer. Once, born on the still, thin air, came the bawl of cattle, easterly.

"What about Injuns?" he asked Nat.

"If the rumor is true they'll probably be up there somewhere."

"You don't act too worried."

Nat reined toward a game trail leading into the foothills. The scorched grass rustled with the passage of his mount. "I'm not," he said. "The one who is supposed to be their leader is an old friend of mine."

Beeton looked back where Russ and his deputy were riding. "Well," he said, "in my country we got Piutes an' they don't have very good memories sometimes. I hope your Apaches are different: from what I've heard they ain't the kindest folks on earth."

They found the abandoned camp with no trouble, and an awkward silence settled around them as they studied it. Finally Russ said, "Those are the tracks of the one I went after. Those must be the other feller's tracks."

They pushed on through a land which was increasingly timbered. The tracks were deeply imprinted for a mile, showing how the fleeing outlaw had dug in, in his hurried flight, then they became less clear, finally, three miles from the camp they veered toward an eminence of shale, and stopped. A broken cigarette showed where the fugitive had squatted, looking back. Here, Sheriff Beeton sent Eggers on ahead. "Best tracker in Nevada," he said to Nat and Russ, by way of explanation. "Funny thing, too, because he ain't a native Westerner. He's from Wisconsin."

"Sure quiet," Nat said.

"Like an Injun; never says much, can shoot like a

marksman an' track like a wolf." Beeton raised his head, studied the still, shimmering slopes around them, and sniffed. "I can almost smell 'em," he said.

They followed in Eggers' wake, riding slowly through the forest-scented atmosphere, grateful for the speckled shade. Up ahead along a ridge dust rose, signaling the coming of a rider. It was Eggers; his face was turkey-red from the heat and his lips were compressed. "Injuns beyond that ridge," he said.

"Did they see you?"

"No; at least if they did they're sure makin' like they didn't. Takin' a siesta by the creek up there."

"How many?"

"Eighteen by my count, all bucks." Eggers removed his hat, flung his head sideways to shake off the sweat, and replaced his hat. "No sign of no white man with 'em, though."

Nat urged his horse out. Beeton watched him ride straight toward the ridge a moment, then he shook his head dolefully and followed after. Russ rode up beside Slim and touched his arm. "Where do the tracks go?" he asked.

"Well, when I seen them Injuns I forgot to look for 'em," the Nevadan said. "Say, does Hendrick know what he's doing? I figure the smartest thing for us to do is get th'hell out of here, quick."

Russ looked sardonic. "You're *too* good a tracker," he said. "Look behind you, on the left there. No, up there east of the ridge."

"Injuns," Eggers breathed softly.

"They've been watching us for the last half hour, Slim. Come on."

Sheriff Beeton was perspiring in rivulets when Nat halted on the ridge, looking down where the Indians were. He mopped his face with a sleeve and wagged his head back and forth. Nat threw back his head and made a long, trilling call. Instantly the Indians down below vanished into the shadows. Nat called a second time, and after a long interval a similar call came back to him. He looked at Beeton, then urged his horse down toward the glade. Before he rode into it, Apaches rose from the shadows around them. Nat paid them slight heed, dismounted, loosened his cinch, and squatted to make a cigarette. Beeton also got down. Slim and Russ acted more stiff and wary when they swung down. A bandy-legged Apache, short and heavy, moved toward them. Others stood back watching, as motionless as stones. "Nan," the Indian said, hunkering across from Nat. "We have been waiting."

He was an older man, this much-feared Apache called Rawgut, with a round and entirely smooth face, full-lipped and kind-appearing. A band of dirty calico crossed his broad forehead to hold back the coarse black hair, and although he wore only a shirt, a breechclout, and high moccasins with *n deh b'keh* buttons that turned up the toes, he seemed to possess dignity. Now, his cloudy brown eyes were serene, even interested, and he seemed an altogether different man from the one called Rawgut about whom so many hair-raising stories were told.

"I knew you would be waiting," Nat said, offering the tobacco sack.

Rawgut took it, made a clumsy cigarette, leaned toward the match. Nat held, and blew out with gusto. His squinted eyes had humor in them. "You want the white man," he said.

"Yes."

Rawgut looked interestedly at Beeton, Eggers, and

Russ—at the stars on their shirt fronts. "The white man is an outlaw."

"Yes."

"*Enju*, Nan."

"Why is it good?" Nat asked.

"Because we could have taken him. We thought he was an outlaw—the way he was hiding—but we did not know."

"So you didn't take him."

"No."

"But you know where he is?"

"Yes. He is not a wise outlaw, Nan. You and I—we could have killed him in his sleep. He is scared, and he is thirsty." Rawgut inhaled mightily and coughed; water filled his eyes. He shook it out and held the cigarette away from his face. "What has he done?"

"Stolen money."

"Ahhh; always money. In Mexico it is money; here it is money." Rawgut smoked a moment. "When your people jump their reservation, Nan, why do they not kill food? Why do they not fill their bellies and lie in the shade? Why is it always money they want?"

"Money buys them food," Nat said. "You know that."

But Rawgut shook his head. "Money buys death, not food," he said. "An outlawed white man cannot ride into villages and buy food—people recognize him—they kill him. An Indian rides into the mountains and kills food; no one cares unless he kills or steals." Rawgut gestured toward the impassive Apaches around them. "These people are also outlaws—because they left the reservation, not because they have stolen or killed—because they need food; they must kill game to take back to their families."

"What about your beef allotment?" Nat asked.

52

Rawgut made a grimace. "Many weeks past due."

Nat's jaw rippled. "Again?"

"Always, Nan, you know that."

"When are you going back?"

Rawgut smiled and made a vague gesture with his fingertips. "There is no hurry."

"They'll send soldiers after you," Nat said.

The smile broadened, real humor showed in the muddy eyes. "You and I have hunted together," Rawgut said. "We know the ways of the animals—we know the ways of the soldiers—there is a big difference, Nan."

"Are you going east?"

"No, I never go east very far; you know that, Nan. I circle around through the mountains and go south."

"Mexico?"

Rawgut made no reply and pushed out his cigarette.

"Listen," Nat said, earnestness making his voice sharp. "You go back. Take the game and go back. I'll see what I can find out about the beef allotment."

"I am not ready."

"Don't go to Mexico," Nat said. "You know what happens down there."

"But they have been our enemies for hundreds of years. They are not your people, Nan."

"I am thinking of *your* people, of what'll happen if you go raiding down there. The soldiers will come, they'll round up your families on the reservation. It'll be like it used to be all over again. Like it was when Geronimo and Natchee and Nana were loose. You remember how that was."

"I remember."

"Then go back."

"We will. We will hunt a little more, we will rest here in the mountains a little more, then we will go back."

Rawgut scratched the ribs under his shirt a moment before he said, "It is good to be here again, Nan. The air is fresh and the shade is good and the water is cold. It is different down there."

"I understand."

"We harm no one being here."

"We have talked about this before," Nat said. "Many times. We know what is right, and we know right is not done. We also know you and I can't change it."

"Yes, we are ants." Rawgut looked for a long time at Nat, then he said, "Do you want the white man today? I will have him brought here."

"Is he close by?"

"Yes." Rawgut turned toward two glittering-eyed younger men, each armed with a Winchester carbine. He spoke in a burst of swift, guttural consonants. The two warriors moved off without replying, and Rawgut faced Nat. "It will not take long. They will not harm him."

"Doesn't he know you're here?" Nat asked.

Rawgut's look of amusement returned. "No," he said. "He has looked at us many times, but he cannot see us. He is watching for white men with large hats riding big horses." Rawgut called for refreshments for his guests. Cold, half-raw venison was brought, along with gourds of cold water. Beeton drank copious amounts of water but ate little of the meat. Eggers was hungry, as was Nat; they both ate well. Russ drank but did not eat. He seemed to be miles away. Rawgut appraised him with sharp, keen attention, but when he spoke to Nat it was about other things.

The high sun slid westerly, and the Apaches went back to drowsing in the shade. Their talk, short and brittle sounding, was interspersed with bursts of

54

laughter. They seemed to have forgotten the four badges sitting in their midst. A yellow haze hung over the mountains, and a stillness lay everywhere but in the glade. Sheriff Beeton finally relaxed, put his carbine aside and made a cigarette. As he exhaled he studied Rawgut. "Where'd you learn English?" he asked.

"I was raised by a white family. I went to school," the Apache said, and fished inside his shirt, bringing out a nearly smooth little medallion, worn about his neck on a thong. "For debating," he said. Beeton bent forward, read the inscription, and looked up at Nat.

"I'll be damned," he said. "He's got a better education than I have."

Nat smiled and Rawgut chuckled. "When you and I sit here on the ground we are alike," he said to Beeton. "It is when I see only your color, and you see only my color, that we are different."

Beeton considered this a moment and nodded. His attention was drawn to the left, where two Apaches were tugging at a disheveled white man whose face was beet-red, his clothing torn and sweat-stiff. The Indians shoved their prisoner toward Rawgut and stood back. Nat looked up at the stranger's wild, protruding eyes, and made a motion for him to sit down. He sank down as though exhausted.

"What's your name?"

"Charley Grieb. I got to have some water."

Russ leaned forward, holding out his half-full gourd. The outlaw took it with shaking hands and drained it.

"What was your pardner's name?"

"Jim Kitchen."

Nat nodded. "I had to be sure," he said. "We've got flyers on both of you. What did you do with the money you got at Duncan?"

55

"Jim took it. He run out on me after some cowboy come bustin' in on us yesterday."

Nat shook his head. "Try the truth next time," he said. "Kitchen's dead—and he had no money on him."

Grieb's checks tightened. A line of pale white shone above his long upper lip. "I don't *know* where it is, lawman. I don't know, and if I did I wouldn't tell you."

Nat drank from his gourd, wiped his mouth and looked at Rawgut. "I'm not allowed to make them talk," he said without emotion, "but I guess there'd be nothing to stop you from doing it, would there?"

"No," Rawgut said, and motioned towards the warriors nearby.

The outlaw's eyes widened and his lips turned gray. "You dassn't," he said to Nat. "Folks'd run you out of the territory . . ."

"Not if they never knew, they wouldn't."

The two Indians put their hands on Grieb's shoulders and he flung away from them with a scream. They fell upon him, pinned him to the ground, holding him there.

"I'll give it to you," the outlaw cried shrilly. "I'll tell you."

"Stand him up."

Grieb sagged between the shorter, more heavily built Apaches, and when Nat signed for them to release him, he fell to his knees. "It's buried," he said. "We cached it after we lit out of Duncan. I'll take you there." Moments later when he regained his composure he stood up, knocked dust from his trousers and said, "And I'll say how you was fixin' to torture me, too. I'll . . ."

"Shut up! Nobody tortured you. There are four of us to swear to that. On your feet." Nat rose, as did his companions. "We'll take him back," he said to the Apache leader. Rawgut nodded and remained silent as the lawmen mounted their horses and started back. Just before they dropped from sight a sinewy, taller-than-average Indian went up and spoke to him. Rawgut listened a moment, glanced up at the sun, which was dipping westerly now, then looked easterly. Finally, he said something to the warrior and they started across the glade toward their companions.

The ride back was through pleasant shade until the forest's edge was reached. There Beeton drew up and sighed, looking out where the dancing heat had curled the grass, burnt it brown. Nat said, "Like a furnace, isn't it?"

Beeton shook the reins and his horse moved out. "Yeah," he said, "but that wasn't what I was thinkin' about. I don't suppose many folks ride into a renegade Injun camp and ride out like we just did. That had me sweatin' worse than the heat." Beeton screwed up his eyes at Nat. "You and him must be old pardners."

"Not exactly," Nat replied. "When I first came to this country I punched cows for the Sabre outfit, over by the Chiricahua Mountains. Met him at a line-camp; his people were on a hunting expedition. I sort of tagged along. We got to be friendly; later, he and I went on a few hunts by ourselves."

"Into Mexico?"

Nat pulled his hat low to shield his eyes as he rode down across the plain. "Well, I wasn't a lawman in those days," he said with a small smile. "Boundary lines didn't mean much to me."

They got back to Gorman's Crossing after sundown, parched, silent, and weary. Russ and Slim Eggers put up the horses. Sheriffs Beeton and Hendrick locked Grieb up, and had no sooner seated themselves in the still dusk of the office than Sheepy came in, furtive-eyed and curious as ever. "Howdy," he said to Nat. "Heard you brung the other one back."

Nat nodded without speaking, and Beeton said, "How's the other guests?"

"Them Pine Tree boys? Meek as Moses," Sheepy said, a twinkle in his eyes. "Their boss come in a little while back and chewed 'em out somethin' fierce. Nary a peep out of 'em."

"Did he fire them?" Nat asked.

"Naw. But right up till the last second I thought he was goin' to." Sheepy's strangely bright eyes went from Nat to Beeton, and back to Nat again. "How long we goin' to hold 'em?" he asked.

"Why?"

"Why? 'Cause they wore me to a frazzle haulin' drinking water in here today, that's why. I never liked havin' drunks in here any time, but this time o' year— just a normal thirst's bad enough, but them fellers with a fire to put out drink water faster'n I can fetch it."

Nat got up and pushed his hat back. "See you later," he said, and went outside. Russ Bell and Slim Eggers were crossing the road from the livery barn. He waited, then started north along the plankwalk with Russ. Just before they got to Betty's café he said, "If you're not doing anything tonight maybe Betty and I'll walk down after supper."

Russ looked down the twilight where his house was for a second before replying. "That'd be fine," he said, and walked on.

Nat watched him for a moment, and pushed into the café. Betty was drawing a cup of coffee, her back to him, when he sat down at the counter. When she turned she glanced briefly into his face and put the cup in front of him.

"Did you get him?"

"Yup."

"Alive?"

Nat's hand, moving toward the cup, grew still. He looked into her handsome face, saw the gray-old wisdom there, and picked up the cup, drank, set it down and sighed. "Alive," he said.

"Did you see any sign of Indians?"

"I guess you could say that. We ate with them. In fact, it was the Indians who brought the outlaw to us."

"That was nice of them," Betty said, turning away.

"Where are you going?"

"To get your supper."

Their eyes held a long moment. Nat took off his hat and dropped it on the bench beside himself. "I told Russ we'd walk down and set a spell this evening."

"All right," Betty said flatly. Moments later when she returned with his meal, her voice was still toneless. "Carrie Lee got up today, Nat."

"Good. You know, Indian women do that. They believe the best way for a . . ."

"You don't understand," Betty said, interrupting. "She's leaving."

Nat put his fork down. "Leaving?"

"She's going to take the baby and go home."

"She can't do that. Why, this heat and the long stage ride would kill 'em both."

"I told her that."

Nat scowled. "Does Doc Simpson know? She'll listen to him."

"He knows. I told him and he went over to talk to her."

"And?"

"He came by shortly before you came back. She told

59

him she'd rather die going home than stay in Gorman's Crossing another day."

Nat's cheeks puffed out and the air went out of him slowly. He got up holding his hat. "Maybe you can tell me what makes women such unreasonable animals," he said. "I'll go clean up and be back. Maybe together we can talk some sense into her."

"All right," Betty said, and watched him disappear into the dusk. Her face was still, her eyes round and wide and expressive.

At the Bell house, Russ washed out on the back porch, then made some supper, meat for himself and porridge for Carrie Lee. The shadows in the bedroom were deep purple, softening the welter of heat. She took the bowl without looking at him, propped herself up and ate. He stood a moment looking at the sleeping baby, listening to its wheezy breath, and said, with his back to her, "We got our man today." Stone-set silence followed. He turned, sat on the edge of the bed and watched her eat. "Remember that dance over at Duncan last summer, Carrie Lee—the one where you tasted that mescal in the lemonade?"

"No!"

He smoothed wrinkles from the skirt of a dress lying across the foot of the bed. "There's some milk in the crock; it's cold. Want some?"

"No."

He got up, stood motionless in the gloom. She put the bowl down and dabbed at her mouth. She hadn't looked at him.

"I'm going home tomorrow," she said, her voice dead and bitter in the darkness. "And I'm going to take the baby."

He went over by the rope-pull and took it in his fists.

60

The clumsy fans began moving. After a time he said, "Is that what you want, Carrie Lee?"

"Yes."

Sweat ran under his shirt. He pulled the rope and let it go automatically, his eyes blind and unseeing. "Well," he said in a flat-toned and discouraged way, "I guess things just didn't work out."

"There's someone on the porch."

He stopped moving, let the rope fall and started out of the room. It was Nat and Betty Aldridge. He let them in and lit a lamp. Their eyes seemed to pierce through him, to read something in foot-high letters written on his soul. He turned away and Betty said, "Have you eaten?"

"Yes. So has Carrie Lee. She's in the bedroom."

Betty started away. Nat fingered his hat a moment, then cast it aside. "Let's set on the porch, Russ." They went outside, where it was ten degrees cooler, and found chairs. "Did she say anything about leaving?" Nat asked.

"Yes. Says she's takin' the boy and going home tomorrow."

"Well, she can't do that," Nat said. "The baby isn't fit to travel yet and it's too hot."

"Doc Simpson said you can't expect reasonableness from her at a time like this, Nat."

"I guess that's right. If she won't save herself then I reckon we've got to do it for her. Take her clothes away, Russ, and I'll ask Betty to stay with her all day tomorrow."

"Nat," Russ said in a hard whisper, "I can't. She isn't a prisoner. I can't treat her like an outlaw—use force on her."

Nat turned his head. "Even to save her life—and the baby's?" Russ didn't answer; his dark profile was sharp

61

against the night and pain lay across it. Several riders went by out on the gravel road, and two strollers came around the edge of the last building, stopped and peered over at the house. Nat recognized them—Beeton and Eggers. "Looks like we're about to have company," he said, watching the two Nevadans pick their way to the gate, pass through it and start up the walk. "I don't think those two ever sleep." Russ stiffened in his chair and started to rise. Nat's voice held him there. "It isn't a social call, not the way they're acting. You better hand and rattle a minute."

The Nevada lawmen stopped at the foot of the porch steps, straining toward the dark shadows above them. Beeton said, "Is that you, Sheriff?"

"Yeah. It's Russ and me. What's on your mind?"

"There's been a killing," Beeton said, and saw Nat draw slowly erect in the chair.

"I didn't hear any shooting."

"Not in town. You'd better come down to the jailhouse."

Nat rose. "What happened?"

"You recollect those Texans with the trail herd? They killed an Injun."

Something very close to dread moved into Nat's eyes.

Come on," he said to Russ Bell, and started down off the porch. Russ followed after, casting a half-bitter and desperate glance at the house.

"How did it happen, Beeton?" Nat asked.

"Seems three, four of them Injuns was lookin' for strayed horses an hour or so ago. One of 'em got too close to that trail herd, one of the drovers seen him and shot him."

"Who brought him in?"

"Two other Injuns. I recognized 'em as some of that

bunch we visited today. I don't think they come voluntarily, though; that big feller, John Summer, and three of his riders is with 'em."

"Summer?" Nat said, puzzled.

"He told me he was comin' back from the river when he heard the shootin' and come onto the Injuns. Said he wouldn't let 'em go back to their tribesmen 'cause he feared what'd happen if the others seen the dead buck."

Nat pushed into the office and Sheepy, pale and puff-eyed from sleep, looked at him without opening his mouth. John Summer and three Pine Tree riders were over by the stove, drinking coffee. Standing above a blanket-shrouded lump on the floor were the two Apaches who had frightened the Duncan outlaw earlier. Their muddy, dark eyes went to Nat's face and clung there, outrage and anger showed in every line of their dark bodies.

John Summer's hand, resting on his holstered gun, dropped to his side. "Evening, Nat," he said calmly, and jutted his chin toward the figure on the floor. "Dead Apache. His friends there say some of 'em were hunting lost horses near that trail herd and some riders shot this one. I was at the river, comin' west, when I heard the shooting. Me and my boys run onto these bucks standing around the dead one and brought 'em in. I figured if they took the dead one back to his people there'd be an Indian uprising over the killing."

Nat knelt, peeled back the blanket and gazed at the corpse, folded the blanket and stood up. He was gazing at the Apaches. "Did you see the shooting?" he asked. One of the Indians shook his head. The other remained silent. "No see, hear. Ride over—find him."

"Why didn't you shoot back?"

"No guns."

Nat's brows lifted. He turned slightly and looked at Summer. "Weren't they armed, John?"

"Nope; all they had was ropes."

"Ropes?"

Russ Bell poured himself a cup of coffee, and over its rim he said, "Maybe to lass' their lost stock, Nat—just as likely to lass' a steer or two. Remember what Rawgut said about them being short on food?"

Nat crossed to the desk and perched on the edge. He frowned. "Rawgut'll go looking for them come dawn. He'll track them to the trail herd."

"An' he'll find blood," Beeton said.

For a while no one said anything. Then one of the Indians bent low, put his hands under the dead man and said, "We go back now."

"You're going to stay here," Nat said. "You take him back and there'll be a war." The Indian made no move to straighten up until he saw the snout of Nat's pistol, then he came erect, with dark blood running in under his cheeks. His companion's slitted eyes were snake-like and venomous. Nat motioned with the gun. "Lock them up, Russ. You go with him, Sheepy." After the Indians had disappeared beyond the cell-block door Nat holstered his hand-gun and swore. "We don't have much time."

John Summer scratched his jaw thoughtfully. "How about turning my riders out?" he asked. "I can't hire a full crew before sun-up, and I don't cotton to the notion of bein' alone at the ranch *after* sun-up."

When Russ and Sheepy returned Nat told his deputy to release the Pine Tree men. Moments later they trooped into the office. At the sight of the shrouded figure on the floor they all halted. Russ got their shell-belts and passed them around without speaking. Finally,

Summer said, "It's a dead Injun; those Texans killed him. We're going back to the ranch and stay close today. No tellin' what's goin' to happen." The cowboys buckled on their guns without speaking, and, except for one or two, avoided looking at either Russ or Nat. Summer crossed the room, stepped over the body and halted at the door. "We'll ride by Maltese Cross," he said to Nat, "and let Ulen know what happened."

After the Pine Tree men had left, Sheriff Beeton made a cigarette, and said in Dakota, "*e Dina sica*; no good. Goin' to be plenty big trouble now, Hendrick."

Nat motioned for Sheepy to get rid of the dead Indian, then he got off the desk and yawned. "Come on, Russ. We got some miles to cover."

"Where you going?" Beeton asked.

"Out to the trail camp. I want to hear the Texas version of this killing."

"That won't change anything, though," the Nevadan said. "The buck's dead—that's all his folks'll care to know."

"But if the killing was justified, I want to know it."

"Mind if me'n Slim tag along?"

Nat faced Beeton. "You fellers've done enough today, and I sure appreciate your help, but you deserve some rest . . . Besides, this time someone's likely to get hurt."

"Well, now, you know I sort of figured that myself," Beeton replied dryly, "and I know for a fact four guns're better'n two. We'll get horses from the barn an' meet you outside. Come on, Slim."

Nat waited until they were gone, then he said to Russ, "Maybe you'd better go tell Doc Simpson what's happened, so he can pass the word along for folks to stay close to town today. I'll get the horses ready." He took four shotguns from the rack and stood a moment, watching old Sheepy dragging the body toward the door. "When you get time, tell the town constable to pass the word around, will you?"

"Sure, Nat." The old man squinted upwards. "You see them Injuns today?"

"Yes."

"Well, I don't know much else," Sheepy said flatly, "but I know Apaches. They'll have their paint-pots out by noon, Nat—whether they find this buck or not. There's nine hundred on the reservation and maybe, out of that number, there's three hundred warriors . . ."

"I know that."

Sheepy grew still. "But I don't believe you ever seen a full-scale Injun uprisin', Nat. Three hundred bronco Apaches takin' up the hatchet is worse'n five thousand Mex soldiers, believe me. They'll lay waste ever' outlyin' ranch, they'll ambush every stage, they'll . . ."

"I didn't come down in the last rain," Nat said sharply, went to the door and passed outside.

Down at the Durelle Saloon, horses hung their heads, drowsing in the dusky coolness, their shadows lying large and grotesque in the roadway beyond. People passing in and out of the doors were caught briefly in the orange lampglow. The night smelled hot and acid-like. Nat drew in a big breath and exhaled slowly. Across the way Beeton and Eggers were sitting their horses, side by side; they looked like statues. Nat went down into the dust and scuffed his way through it, lugging the four shotguns. Behind him came the hurrying ring of Russ Bell's spurs.

CHAPTER 5

THEY RODE THROUGH THE FAINT MOONLIGHT WITHOUT speaking until a crooked ribbon of silver shone ahead. Nat told Beeton they were nearing the Santa Clara River. The Nevadan grunted. "That's the most water, outside of sweat, I've seen in Arizona. Is the herd around here some place?"

"It's suppose to be. At least, the last time I talked to Hays I told him about the grass and water over here."

Slim Eggers raised his head, sniffing. After a moment he said, "I don't smell any cattle."

Ahead of them, like crumpled dark cardboard, the mountains loomed high and ageless. Where the river wound southward moonlight lay upon its oily surface, and when they got closer there was a tangled growth of willows and cottonwoods along it. "Slim," Beeton said, "ride on ahead and see if you can find a trail to the water."

Eggers hadn't been gone twenty minutes when a solitary gunshot shook the darkness. Nat lifted his horse into a gallop and, followed by Beeton and Russ Bell, he loped north along the river's edge until he saw a rider sitting in the willows up ahead. It was Eggers and he was agitated. "No wonder they potted that Apache," he said tightly when the others came up and stopped. "They're night-guarding like an army."

"Where are the cattle?"

"Cussed if I know," Eggers said. "Probably yonder up the river a ways yet. But they're guardin' way down here."

"Did you see anyone?"

"Just one. He was sittin' his horse in the willows

when he shot at me. Then he high-tailed it north."

"Come on," Nat said, leading off.

"You're goin' to ride into a slug," Eggers protested, but he fell in beside Russ and loped along.

Beeton, riding stirrup with Nat, was worried. "Listen, Sheriff, they're bound to think it's more Injuns and you can't blame 'em for shooting first."

Nat threw back his head and called out. The echo reverberated through the night and bounced off the mountains. He called twice more, then, far out, there was an answer. Nat drew down to a walk and rode toward it. "It's customary," he told Beeton, "to sing out before you shoot at someone in the dark. These fellers are pretty quick with their trigger-fingers."

"Yeah, but they just had Injun trouble."

"That's what I'm talking about," Nat said. "Neither Summer or those Apaches said they called out before they killed that buck."

A lantern's faint glow showed westerly from the river. Nat rode toward it, and he called out again, saying who he was. A few minutes later a shadow came off the ground in front of his horse. The Texan had a carbine in both hands; without speaking he motioned them forward. Later, when they reined up where the lantern was, a second lanky figure appeared out of the gloom. It was Willard Hays, with a carbine cradled in his arm. "Thought you was an Injun," he said to Nat.

"Lucky for you we weren't," Nat said, dismounting. What happened out here tonight?"

"Some Injuns come a-skulkin' around, trying to run off a few head. We got one of 'em, but by the time we snuck up where he got shot, his friends'd packed him off."

"You got him all right," Nat said. "He was riddled.

68

Why didn't you holler out before you started shooting?"

Hays' hard eyes grew very still. "Sure. We should've hollered out an' brought every cussed Injun 'thin five miles down on us. Not likely, Sheriff. Y'know, us Texas boys been raised in Comanche country. We grow up learnin' to shoot first and holler afterwards." Hays surveyed Beeton, Eggers and Bell, then put his carbine butt-down and leaned on it. "Why're you so all-fired het up, anyway? It was just an Injun."

"I live here," Nat said sharply. "You fellers are just passing through. You kill an Apache and start an Indian war, then you ride on. The rest of us have to stay here and do the fighting."

"Well," Hays said, the edge leaving his voice, "if you want, me and a couple of my boys'll go 'Pache hunting with you."

Nat ignored the offer. "You sure keep a big night-watch," he said. "One of your men fired on Eggers here, a full mile from the herd."

"We don't take no chances at night. We all ride nighthawk, then spell off sleepin' during the day."

"It's usually done the other way around," Nat said.

"Mebbe; but me, I'm different. Specially when I'm in unfriendly country, Sheriff. I keep the whole crew nighthawking. That's my practice."

Sheriff Beeton, who had been watching Hays and listening, now said, "When did you leave Fort Hall?"

"About a month back."

"An' you trailed east along the Blackfoot River?"

"Yep."

Beeton sat back in the saddle, gazing steadily at the Texan. "Where are the rest of your men?"

Hays made a sweeping gesture with one arm. "Out yonder, waitin' for another Injun."

69

Nat toed into the stirrup and sprang up. "Hays," he said coldly, "you better get that herd on the move. We'll be coming back this way sometime tomorrow and I don't want to find you here."

Hays' expression grew stiff and unpleasant. For a moment words lay on his lips, then he turned abruptly and walked away without speaking. Beeton watched him disappear. "I've seen that feller some place, Hendrick. I've been rackin' my brains, but for the life of me I can't recollect where."

Nat spun his horse and started north again. He didn't stop until the land began to lift under his horse, then he let the others come up. "Make plenty of noise," he said. "We don't want Rawgut's band to think we're trying to surprise them."

It took hours of slow riding to reach the shale-ridge from which Eggers had first seen the Indians, and when they started down the far side toward the glade, Nat called out several times. The only answer he got was an eerie echo.

The glade was empty.

Nat dismounted and poked among the cooking-fires. They were cold. Russ Bell came up with some discarded rags and said, "They've been gone quite a while, Nat. I'd guess since about sundown."

"I don't like it," Nat replied.

"Maybe they took your advice and started back."

"No. They'd have waited until morning. Indians rarely travel at night, unless they're . . ."

"Yeah," Russ said thinly, "unless they're going on a raid."

Beeton came forward scratching his head and scowling. "You know, Hendrick, on a still night like this the sound of a rifle-shot could carry for miles. I don't expect they know what happened to their friend, but I'll bet a good horse they heard the shots that killed him."

"Then they'll be down there watching the trail herd, hunting for their companions—the ones I locked up in town."

Eggers said, "How come 'em to let us ride past?"

"Ain't hard to figure that one," Beeton said. They can cut us off that way."

Nat went back to his horse and mounted. "Come on, we've got a lot of riding to do to get around them and back down on the range."

They rode northwest through the darkness until an elongated spur of mountain left them sitting far above the mottled stage road down below. Nat studied the pale land. "I guess we'd better get back to town and get a posse," he said in a lifeless tone. "I'd hoped we'd find Rawgut so I could talk him out of doing anything rash."

"Ever try out-shouting the wind?" Beeton asked wryly.

After they got down to the stage road the going was easier, but the closer they got to Gorman's Crossing the more despondency settled over Nat. They passed the four o'clock stage two miles north of town, and Nat told Beeton he didn't think the stage-line officials had been impressed with his suggestion that folks stay close by until the trouble was past. Beeton concurred and made a remark about people whose lives ran by schedules.

When they got back Russ left briefly to see his wife. Nat sent Sheepy out to round up a posse among the cowboys still stomping down the dark hours at the saloon, then poured a pan of cold water to wash his face in. Moments later, while he was drying, Betty Aldridge came in. Beeton and Eggers looked startled, and Nat, finished drying, tossed the towel aside.

"What's the matter?" he asked.

"Carrie Lee was on the four o'clock stage," she said. "I was with her until after midnight, when she fell asleep. I went home, Nat. Just a little while ago Doctor Simpson came by and told me he'd called on his way home, and she was gone—she and the baby."

They were all standing there, absorbing what they knew, when the door burst in and Russ filled the entrance, his face gray, and his eyes wide. "She's gone," he said.

"Betty just told us," Nat said, in as calm a tone as he could muster. "She must've been on that stage we passed."

"I'm going after her."

"Wait a minute, Russ."

"Wait for what? Those Apaches are out there!" Russ spun around. The door was closing when Nat's voice, a toplash of sound, stopped him.

"*Hold it!* If the Apaches want that stage they'll have it by now. Think! We saw that stage over an hour ago and it was traveling fast. Even if you caught it this side of Duncan, which you couldn't, and even if you did get to it ahead of the Indians—what could you do, one man and one gun?"

"That's *my* wife and *my* baby on there," Russ shouted, all color draining from his face.

"And going off half-cocked is what made you kill that unarmed outlaw, too," Nat said without mercy. "Now you go help Sheepy round up a posse down at the saloon, then you come back here and ride with the rest of us." His tone softened. "Don't make another mistake today, Russ."

Bell slammed the door. Beeton went to an open box of shotgun shells and put a handful into his shirt pocket.

72

"He'll come through all right," he said. "It takes things like this, sometimes, to make a boy grow into a man overnight." He motioned Eggers forward. "Better take an extra pocket full of these things, Slim. Nothin' wilts Injuns like a scattergun up close."

Betty was watching Nat in silence. Finally she turned, went to the door, and said, "Good luck, Nat. I'll have something for you to eat when you get back."

After she had gone Sheriff Beeton kept looking after her. Finally he said, "You fixing to marry that girl, Hendrick?"

"Yes, why?"

"If you wasn't I'd sure like to try. How many womenfolk you ever seen that know a man's goin' out and maybe get killed, who just say they'll have supper ready when you get back?"

"Not many. Come on. No, not you, Sheepy. You stay here and watch things."

"Why, blast you," the old man said, red-faced and angry, "I've lifted more Apache topknots than you've ever seen!"

"I believe you, but someone dependable's got to watch the prisoners, too."

The posse consisted of four townsmen and six half-drunk cowboys. Beeton grinned as he mounted. "They'll be as sober as judges as soon as the hot sun hits 'em," he told Eggers. "Nothing like a good fry to sweat the alky out of a man's bones."

The posse rode straight for the Texas trail herder's camp, and when they got to the Santa Clara, heading north, and weren't challenged, Nat had forebodings. Where the wagon stood, slatternly looking and forlorn under the smoke yellow crescent of moon, Nat raised his voice several times without receiving a reply.

73

During one moment of silence Beeton asked Eggers if he'd ever tracked Indians by moonlight. The deputy said he had not.

Nat rode across the foothills seeking a trail of bent grass. Finding nothing, he reasoned the Apaches would not travel far with their captive Texans. They halted to off-saddle and await dawn, near a crooked trill of water known as Grave Creek. His possemen lay down in the grass and, except for three of the cowboys, all were silent.

"Bet they'll raid Maltese Cross," one rider said, almost gleefully.

"If they do," a second voice said in equally thick tones, "they'll think they got Old Scratch hisself by the tail."

"Aw," scoffed another voice, "Fritz'd never know what hit him. Apaches is smart—they're real *coyote*, as the Mexes say—real *coyote*."

"Bet they'll catch the stage, too. You fellers ever see what they do to folks when they're on the rampage?"

Russ, sitting beside Nat, who was leaning against his saddle watching the crystal clear wash of stars overhead, drew stiff and taut.

"Well, sir, once, down by Sonora, I seen a wagonload of Mexes they used up, an' I'm here t'tell you . . ."

Nat's voice went flat and sharp across the night. "Shut up. You better rest while you can because when it's light enough you'll need all the guts you're wasting now talking."

Silence fell. Sullen but obedient silence. After a time one of the townsmen asked in a sober voice if Nat didn't think the Apaches would make for Mexico.

"No. You see, I talked to Rawgut yesterday, and he knows that's where I'll expect him to go. I think he'll go

74

east, over towards Dura Canyon."

"They got mescal pits up there some place," one of the cowboys said. "I come across 'em last year when I was hunting strays. If they get over there and get a heat on, I wouldn't want to be their captive."

Beeton interrupted to ask something which had long been bothering him. "You know, Piutes wouldn't have acted like this. They'd have crept up close enough to shoot those Texans, then they'd have faded away. What d'you reckon made these Injuns take those Texans alive?"

"I've got an idea," Nat replied. "Rawgut doesn't know—or *didn't* know—what became of the horse-hunting party. All he knew, probably, was that they were supposed to come back, and they didn't. And maybe, like you said, he heard the shooting. I know Rawgut pretty well; he's not a blood-thirsty Apache like the older ones were. He'd want to make sure of what happened before he took up the hatchet."

"So you figure he slipped up on those Texans maybe one at a time, and captured them alive?"

"Correct. The next question is: can we get to them before he tortures the truth out of them? If we don't . . ."

"No Texans," Russ said. "And I don't feel sorry for them. Not one damned bit."

False dawn came a little later and Slim Eggers made a scout for tracks. He found them, alerted the posse, and led them at a loose gallop along the foothills, westerly. "This is a new route to me," Nat told Russ. "Where do you reckon they're heading?"

"Maybe along the flank of the mountains to Turner's Gap, then around into Badwater Valley."

Russ's guess proved correct. The sun had been up an hour when Eggers got down and poked down among

75

broken weeds at his feet. "They rested here," he said. "I'd say they aren't more'n an hour ahead." Another hour later, when they were riding through the jagged rock country of Turner's Gap, Nat pointed out fresh horse droppings. Russ sniffed and said, "You can still smell the dust. Not much farther now."

Beeton cast a critical look at the vertical lift of mountains ahead of them. He said, "If I was trying to pick a place to bushwhack somebody, this'd be the spot."

Turner's Gap was a choked-up canyon of barren rock. A permanent twilight lay in its depths and some scrubby brush grew along a very faint game-trail that climbed ever higher among the boulders. Nat knew the country, knew what lay behind. He also knew that if Rawgut's Apaches had turned hostile, they would wipe out his posse as soon as it got down into that canyon. One of the cowboys said, "I ain't goin' in there, and if the rest of you got a lick of sense you won't either."

Nat balanced his knowledge of Rawgut against the imminent peril and lifted his reins. The horse went forward obediently and Sheriff Beeton, next in line, pushed sweat off his face, thrust his feet forward, and sighed. "Go on, horse," he said. "The best part of your life's behind you, too."

Eggers followed and Russ, balancing a shotgun across his lap, went next. His eyes, narrowed against the heat, roved the cliff faces on either side. The others trailed after, just as grim-faced as Russ, and the last man to enter the Gap was the cowboy who had said he would not: the profanity he used to bolster a badly frightened spirit was the only man-made sound.

The horses picked their way around boulders and through shale. Tiny landslides rattled down. The air

76

grew cooler, but no one noticed it. To Nat the trail, winding upwards, seemed endless. Each weighty second felt like an eternity. Then a cloud which had appeared from nowhere obscured the yellow sun, and shadows piled down into the canyon, layer upon layer. Nat looked at the sky. There were other clouds there, and the air gradually took on a metallic scent and taste. "Summer thundershower coming," he said to Beeton.

"That'll be nice," the Nevadan replied. "Specially if we're in this blasted canyon when it hits."

"We won't be."

They reached the rim of the canyon after an hour's ride. Nat halted to study the land ahead, and to "blow" the horses. Beeton made a cigarette, lit it, looked back and shook his head. When Russ came up beside him he said, "I could afford to lose the ten pounds I worried off down there, but I can think of better ways of gettin' rid of fat, Deputy."

Russ spurred up beside Nat. "Slim says they can't be more'n a mile ahead. If we stay up here they'll see us."

"I want them to. I don't want to fight Rawgut, I want to talk to him."

"Do you think he'll have all his bucks with him?"

Reading Russ's mind right then was not difficult. "I hope so," Nat said, swivelling in the saddle to see if all the riders were up. "Come on," he said to Russ. "I'd like to get this done before nightfall." As his horse moved out Nat added, "We can't risk going back through the Gap—not with a thunderstorm coming."

The cursing cowboy began to complain about the lack of water. Nat handed his canteen back without a word. When it came back it was empty. He made a face at Russ and led them across a wind-scourged plateau devoid of any kind of vegetation. Slim Eggers jogged past, eyes on the ground. Where the trail started down toward a shallow, brawling creek, he halted and pointed. "They're down along that creek somewhere. Probably where it cuts back into the trees yonder."

"How do you know?"

Eggers lifted his head. "No dust," he said. "If they were going up the other side of the valley there'd be dust."

Nat considered only briefly. He knew enough about Apaches to be sure that if Rawgut had meant to ambush him, he would have done it back in the canyon. That he had not made Nat bold. He led the posse down toward the creek. Four of his possemen fell off their horses to lie flat and suck water, which burst out of their pores almost instantly, making them less comfortable than before. Nat and Russ drank side by side, and the sheriff refilled his canteen. The water was clear, but, because the creek-bed was shallow, it tasted tepid. "Water your horses," Nat said, and went over where Eggers was standing, watching his mount drink.

"I'm going up the creek a ways. If they're going to shoot it's better they shoot one man instead of twelve or fourteen. The rest of you stay here and don't shoot no matter what happens, until I get back."

"I understand," Eggers said. He lifted his arm and pointed. "See where that big fir tree is, over by that black rock? Well, that's about where you'll find 'em."

Nat talked briefly with Russ and Beeton, then mounted and started forward, following the thicket-course of the creek. Except where his horse's hooves struck stone, the little glade along the creek was steeped in silence. When he had a good glimpse of the fir tree Eggers had referred to, he halted and made a high, trilling, Apache call. The hush, unnaturally deep, stifled his echo and there was no reply. He made the call again, then a doubt began to grow in him. Finally, where the violent sun burned along a ragged lip of rock, he caught a blur of movement. He dismounted, kept his horse between him and the fir tree, and tried again to call. This time a shot rang out in reply, thunderous and flat in the heavy atmosphere. An Apache appeared upon the ragged rim, squatting. His shirt-tail hung around the bent, stringy legs and the arms holding the carbine lay relaxed across his knees. He made no move to hide or avoid being seen, and he kept his face toward Nat. His hair, held back by a limp circlet of red calico, showed as glinting black as a crow's feathers.

"Rawgut!" Nat called.

The sentinel raised his carbine carefully, took long aim but did not fire. In his native tongue he shouted, "Go back, white eyes. Go away."

"I want to talk to Rawgut."

This time the sentry replied in reservation-English. "No talk. Too much talk already. Now you go back." The carbine lifted again, motionless, with the sun's hot rays running like fire along its barrel.

"You've got to call Rawgut."

"*No!*"

Nat could see the finger curling around the trigger. "I've got Apaches to trade," he said in loud desperation. I've got Indians to give Rawgut."

The sentry's gun went down a fraction, but the malevolent eyes behind it did not soften. "You lie!"

"I've got two Apaches locked up at Gorman's Crossing. I want to trade them for your prisoners."

The sentry's head whipped around at some sound Nat could not hear. A second Indian appeared among the rocks. Nat recognized him with a sigh of relief.

79

"Rawgut! I've come to trade you two Apaches for the Texans you've got."

"Where are they, Nan?" came the hard and reproving reply.

"Back in town at the jailhouse. Listen, Rawgut—"

"Nan, you are lying to an old friend. You have no live Apaches."

"Who told you that?"

"My prisoners. They told us they killed one man— but they did a lot of shooting and *three* men are missing."

"A white rancher found your other two men standing over the warrior the Texans killed. He brought all three to me, in town."

"Hah! No white rancher takes three Apaches captive. You know better than that, Nan."

"He had cowboys with him. He brought all three to me."

"Why?"

"So your men wouldn't go back to you with the dead man before I had a chance to talk to you. Listen, Rawgut, we don't want to fight you."

"I have lost men. You know I cannot return while they lie unavenged." Rawgut stood up in plain sight. "Three of my men have gone for reinforcements already. I did not bring this thing between us, Nan, but it is there."

"Send someone to stop the men who have left. Let me give you the two live Apaches for the Texans. White-man law will take care of them."

"Who will take care of the dead men's families? Who will bring back their bodies from your town? Who will make my people believe you don't want war?"

"Rawgut, there isn't . . ."

80

"Go back, Nan. Take your posse and go back. I wouldn't let you be killed in the canyon, but if you stay here I cannot protect you further. I am one man; I brought these men here to get food; whites have killed three of them for no reason; you are an old friend to me—but not to the others. If you remain I cannot stop them; they will kill all of you. Now go back, Nan, and if you would come again, bring the bodies of the slain."

CHAPTER 6

NAT RETURNED TO THE OTHERS, AND BEETON, SEEING his face, swore to himself. The cowboys and townsmen clustered around him in silence, their faces asking the same question. Nat swung down wearily. "Russ, I want you to do something. Take six of these men and ride east toward the reservation. Where the trail leading down into the San Carlos leaves the hills, lay an ambush, and when Rawgut's reinforcements come up off the reservation, turn them back."

"Kill them?"

"If you have to, yes, but first shoot the horses from under them. I want them to think half an army's between them and Rawgut's band."

One of the cowboys said, "That won't stop 'em, Sheriff. They'll go back down to the valley and skirt the foothills until they get west of the river, then they'll · come up behind us."

Nat studied the rider a moment before he said, "Do you know where the Maltese Cross is?"

"Sure; used to work for Fritz. Why?"

"You ride there and tell Ulen to make for the foothills."

81

"I understand. You want him between you and Rawgut."

"No. I want him to hide in the hills until the hostiles have gone past, then I want him to trail them—without letting them see him, and without fighting them."

The men, including Sheriff Beeton, were scowling. Russ said, "What about Pine Tree? They're closer, Nat."

"That's right." Nat picked out one of the townsmen. "You ride for Summer's place and get him to take his crew into the hills south of where we are now. He's to string the men out, and when the hostiles come up, he's to open fire on them like Russ's men are going to do—set them afoot if he can, without killing them."

Beeton's face cleared. "A surround," he said. "I get it. Maltese Cross will be behind them, Pine Tree in front, and the Injuns'll be afoot."

Nat nodded. "And the rest of us'll be up here blocking Rawgut's band from getting through the canyon to his friends." Nat put a hand on Russ's arm, said nothing, and let his hand drop away. "Go on, boys."

As they were watching the men leave, Sheriff Beeton said, "If this works it'll be good strategy. Only it looks to me you're goin' way out of your way not to kill Injuns."

"There's been too much killing already," Nat replied. "I think it's time we figured out ways to stop the killing, not continue it." He mounted his horse and led the remainder of the posse, himself, Beeton, Eggers, and three others, back to the top of the canyon. There, well back from the basalt rim, they all dismounted. They were on the highest eminence and no one could look down on them. Nat gave his reins to Beeton with orders for each man to stand close to his horse and be prepared to cut off any nicker the animals might make, then he

82

moved forward toward the plateau's rim. Rawgut would send a scout to make sure the white men had withdrawn. He would probably trail them, and Nat meant to meet him as he came up the trail from the creek.

The sun beat down mercilessly. Where Nat lay, flat on his stomach against the flinty earth, watching the trail to the creek, hot silence reigned. Beyond his vantage point the land fell sharply toward the glade. Down there a woodpecker's beat echoed in rocketing waves of sound. Scanning the creek's courseway, Nat saw an Indian move out of the willows with quick, wild movements, trot toward the trail and start up it. He watched the buck come on, stopping now and then to study the hoof-patterns before him. Once he whipped erect, staring at the rim above him. Nat held his breath; the pounding of his heart sounded like thunder. Then the Apache started upwards again, moving in a loose, easy crouch, his legs glistening with sweat, working with tough ease. Fifty feet from where Nat lay, legs drawn up to spring, the Indian halted again, as though sensing another presence. He moved closer and halted again. This time the premonition seemed stronger; he dropped to his knees, hands flat against the hot shale, as though to lunge ahead. He did not move from that position for a full minute, his cloudy black eyes ranging along the rim above.

Nat's pistol-butt was slippery in his fist. He, too, was prepared to spring. Then the Apache started forward once more, moving more slowly and still crouched. He could not see beyond the rim, but he was straining to do so. Nat heard the whisper of sound where his mocassins made their way over the shale, and as the Indian leapt over the rim to land crouched, Nat sprang. The Apache saw him at once and jerked erect, one hand flashing for the knife in his belt. Nat's gun made a short, flashing arc. It struck the Apache in the chest and knocked him down. He tried to roll away from the white man's larger body, but he was stunned. Then he opened his mouth to cry a warning and Nat pushed his hand into his face.

It required only a moment to truss the Apache's hands behind him. Nat squatted, holstered his pistol, and sucked in great gulps of air. Tiny bursts of light exploded in front of his eyes for a moment.

When the Apache began to squirm Nat lifted him, shoved him along, and went back to where the others were. Sheriff Beeton was making a cigarette. He stopped long enough to survey the sweaty prisoner, then popped the thing into his mouth. Nat said, "Don't light it. Apaches can smell tobacco smoke a mile away."

"All right. Mean-lookin' little cuss, ain't he? Will they send any more?"

"Not for a long time," Nat replied. "Not until they're satisfied something's happened to this one."

The Apache hunkered in the shade of a saddle-horse and would not look into the faces of his captors. Nat knelt beside him and asked what had been done with the Texans. The Indian would not reply. Nat put a hand on the sinewy shoulder and shook. The Apache glared at him, and after a moment, he said something in his native tongue. Nat removed his hand and stood up. "Just our luck to get one that doesn't speak English. Keep an eye on him. I'll go back and make sure Rawgut doesn't send another one."

"Wait a minute," Eggers said. "How will we know when them other fellows are between us and the other Injuns?"

"Simple," Nat said. "You'll hear shooting." He looked at the sun a moment. It wasn't quite directly overhead. "I think they ought to be in place by noon. If Russ turns the Indians back they ought to be around here by about two o'clock."

"Sure a lot of ifs," Eggers said in a low tone.

Nat continued to study the sky. Finally, addressing Beeton, he said, "I think that thunderstorm's going to hold off until tonight, Sheriff. Maybe we can use the canyon to get back out of here, after all."

"Yeah; *if* we get back out of here."

Nat returned to the basalt rim and lay flat. Down by the creek there was movement. Evidently Rawgut, feeling secure, felt no further need for hiding. He and his remaining warriors were watering their horses and talking. Only occasionally did one look upwards. Nat's attention was caught by the sight of four white men, bareheaded and brush-scratched. The Indians treated them with casual cruelty, and when one of them asked for water, all four were shoved head-first into the stream. The Indians laughed at their spluttering groans and finally pulled them out by the ropes binding their arms behind them. Rawgut squatted in front of his prisoners. For a while he studied them in silence, then he began speaking. Nat could not hear his words, but he could see the faces of the Texans, which was enough. Then Hays, his mahogany-colored features drawn tight with fear and hatred, made a short, nasal reply, and Nat heard the words easily.

"It wasn't us—we seen the sheriff from Gorman's Crossin' do it. He shot the other two and lugged 'em away." Again Rawgut spoke. Hays' reply sounded clear in the stillness. "Sure, he tied 'em across their horses and went back to town."

Rawgut's arm moved in a blur. Nat saw Hays' head slam back from the blow. Then Rawgut was speaking

85

again, and anger made his voice shrill enough for the words to carry. "You lie! We found one horse. If Nan had taken them all back tied over their horses, we would not have found a horse."

The captive Nat recognized as the cook spoke to Hays in a whining-frightened tone. "Tell him the truth, Will. F'gosh sakes don't get him mad."

Hays' face was suffused with dark blood, his slitted eyes showed fire-points of fury. He had trouble controlling his voice when next he spoke. "All right, one of your bucks got shot. We don't know what happened to the others. We snuck up real slow, in case there was more around. By the time we got where the shooting took place, all we found was plenty blood and some tracks. Some of the horses was shod, some was barefoot."

"You read the sign . . ."

"Yeah, we read it. Looked like some whites come along found the dead Injun an' maybe a couple other Injuns, and took 'em all away."

"Away, where?"

"South, towards Gorman's Crossing."

"Alive?"

"How would we know?"

"You heard no shooting?"

Hays shook his head. "After my men shot, there was no more shooting."

Rawgut continued to stare at the Texan. He rocked back on his heels. "Why did you shoot my hunter?"

"To protect my cattle."

Rawgut fell silent again, and after a while he stood up. Several of his men who were standing near spoke. Rawgut listened, then moved off without replying. Nat saw the Apaches stare after him. He knew that unless

Rawgut made a show of taking vengeance for the dead and missing men, his warriors would depose him and exact their own revenge: Apache leadership hinged upon a chieftain's ability to wage successful warfare, and his willingness to follow Apache custom.

Rawgut went along the creek to a place where three bucks were cooking torn chunks of beef over a pencil-thin fire of punk-wood—which made no smoke. There he dropped down upon a red cowhide and began eating. After a while, drawn by the scent of cooking red meat, other Apaches came up and squatted. Very little was said. When Rawgut finished eating one of the other Indians tossed him a white tassel of cowhide. Nat watched him examine the thing, heft it, and shove it into his waistband. It was one of the extra-long dewlaps from one of Hays' critters.

A scraping of sound behind Nat made him whirl. Beeton was crawling up beside him, sweat dripping from his chin and nose. He went flat, sucking in air. "Any more comin' up here?"

"No; they're eating."

"Buck-meat?"

"One of Hays' critters. I think Russ was right. Those bucks weren't looking for lost horses, they were scouting up some Texas beef."

"More power to 'em," the Nevadan said in a coarse whisper. "Too bad they didn't run off the whole blessed herd. It'd have kept 'em too busy to make trouble."

"Might be a good idea," Nat said, "to send one of our boys back along the rim where he can see down into the canyon or out across the range. He can let us know when Summer or the other Indians get close."

"I'll take care of it," Beeton said, edging back from the rim. "Whew, it's hotter'n blue blazes up here. I'd give a gee-gaw to waller in that creek for a spell." As he was getting to his knees, Beeton looked at Nat. "How many are down there?"

"Twelve."

"Hmmm. When we visited with 'em I counted eighteen. Do you reckon he sent some of 'em to intercept that stage?"

"1 doubt it. I think the rest went back to San Carlos to round up reinforcements."

"Sure hope you're right." Beeton's gaze lingered. "You pretty sure Bell'll do like you said? I mean, he won't leave the others and try to find out about his wife and kid, will he?"

"What do you think?"

Beeton got slowly to his feet, dusted off his clothing and said, "No, I don't think he'd do that."

After the Nevadan was gone Nat resumed his vigil. The Indians had finished eating. Some led their horses into the creek and splashed water over them. Several others curled up in the shade and slept. Four went over where the Texans were and sat watching them in stony silence. Rawgut and another Apache engaged in conversation.

After a while Nat rolled over onto his back and squinted skyward. The sun was slightly off-center. He thought John Summer should be in place by now, and Russ should have turned Rawgut's reinforcements. As the minutes crept by, doubts began to assail him. If something went wrong he had led a number of men into a bad spot. Finally, unable to stand the strain, he edged back and got to his feet. He was starting back when Beeton returned, his face red and sticky.

"Summer's in place down there. I went to have a look, myself."

"How many men?"

"They're hid, but I counted twelve. Maybe another four or five I didn't see." Beeton looked critical. "You know, we're between him and Rawgut's band, an' if them other Apaches got around Summer, we'll be between two bands of roiled up Injuns—not a good place to be."

"There's that chance," Nat said, walking back across the plateau with Beeton trailing after him. At the far edge of land one of the townsmen was squatting, motionless. He got up as Nat came along, and without speaking he pointed downwards. Nat saw the dustcloud before Beeton did. "That should be Rawgut's reinforcements."

"Or the Maltese Cross," the townsman said.

"Nope, it's Injuns all right." Beeton pointed farther east. "There's your Maltese Cross; that other dust-banner way back there."

"Come on," Nat said. "We've got some work to do." Back where the others were standing by the captive Apache, Nat grouped them. "Now, the firing'll begin pretty quick, and Rawgut's sure to hear it. He'll send scouts out, and maybe only one or two'll use the trail. The others'll go east and west of us around the plateau. Two of you will ride east and get set in the rocks. When you see a mounted Apache put him afoot. You, Eggers, and the man next to you. Beeton and I'll go along the west rim of the flat and watch for Apaches threading through Turner's Gap. If we see any we'll do the same."

"Yeah," Eggers said, "but what if they go north?"

"Let 'em. North is away from Gorman's Crossing and the cow country. They won't find anything in that direction but five hundred miles of damned hard riding—and mountains. All right, Eggers, you two go

89

on. Whatever you do, hide your horses."

Beeton watched the two men ride off. He mopped his face and hitched up his pants. He and Nat Hendrick went to the plateau's westerly rim, which commanded an excellent view of the dark canyon below, and there Nat back-tracked so he could watch the trail leading upwards from the creek. "Watch your step," he said to the Nevadan. "They can hear rocks falling farther than we can."

Beeton sank down with both hands on his carbine. He tilted his hat forward and peered downwards. "By grannies," he said, "I admire what you're tryin' to do, Hendrick, but it can't be done. Them Injuns're out to kill, and it just follows we're goin' to kill a few."

"They won't kill anybody if you set them afoot," Nat said. He was going to say more when the distant, soft pop of gunfire came to him. He twisted around and looked down into the glade where the Apaches were. Several were standing motionless, heads on one side. Rawgut twisted away from his horse and stood stiff and taut. The sleeping Apaches came awake as though by instinct. They got to their feet with supple grace and moved over near Rawgut. One of the Texans spoke and an Indian, walking past, turned and kicked him, then resumed his passage toward the gathering knot of men around the leader. Rawgut gestured for silence. The sound of gunfire, faint as it was, increased in volume. After placing its location, Rawgut spoke rapidly to his men. In a moment the Indians had their prisoners on horses and were herding them ahead, toward Turner's Gap. Nat's lips drew back in a mirthless smile. He wasn't the only one who thought there would be no ambush.

When the Apache mounts cat-walked toward the

Gap's faint game-trail, Sheriff Beeton lay flat and craned his neck to see. "Ain't a one of 'em comin' up the plateau trail," he told Nat. "They're driving the Texans ahead, to stop bullets first, I expect."

"When they're in range, down their horses."

"Yeah, then what do we do? They'll come swarmin' up this sidehill like ants."

"We won't be here."

Beeton grunted and edged his carbine up, snugged it back against his shoulder and waited. After a time he said, very softly, "I got one in range." He fired and Nat saw the Indian's horse tumble off the trail and go sliding down through the shale, setting free a small avalanche. At once the other Apaches fought their horses around. Nat selected a target and dumped another horse. The rider went with him, rolling and twisting down the canyon's wall. A startled dark face swung upwards. Nat was aiming when Beeton's carbine exploded a second time. The Apache, as agile as a cat, flung himself free as his mount fell and rolled. The Indians began crying out to one another, and the Texans, following the lead of Willard Hays, urged their frightened mounts on along the trail. Hays was guiding his horse by knee pressure. The Indians were too concerned for their own safety to remember the prisoners.

"How about them?" Beeton said, pointing with his carbine toward the escaping men.

"Let them go. Summer'll pick them up when they come out of the canyon."

Rawgut was with the main band. He now led them in a reckless race back down toward the creek. Nat took long aim and fired; it was a miss. "Out of range," Beeton opined, reloading his gun. "Anyway, we turned 'em back, and they got no more hostages."

91

Nat crawled along the rim on all fours, watching the Indians. As soon as they got back by the creek they abandoned their horses, in typical Apache fashion, and melted into the shadows. By the time Beeton came up, there wasn't an Apache in sight anywhere. "Now what'll they do?"

"Either go north into the mountains, which is straight uphill, or east around the plateau. Come on, we'll figure they're going to try the other way, around the plateau." They trotted through the blazing heat until they found Eggers and his companion behind some man-high rocks.

Nat had guessed correctly. The Indians, no longer mounted, came wraith-like through the heat waves, seeking a way past their attackers. "No horses," Beeton said, "so I expect we pot Injuns."

"In the legs."

All three men turned to gaze at Nat. He did not speak and finally they resumed their vigil. It was impossible to tell whether Rawgut's entire band was down below where sage and greasewood thickets dotted the slope, or whether only part of the band was there. Until Nat saw Rawgut himself, he wondered; afterwards, he knew all the dissidents were down there. Again he tried a long shot at Rawgut, and again he missed. Beeton was more fortunate. When his gun went off a lithe figure leapt straight into the air from the heart of a thicket, and fell back amid the thorny limbs with much threshing. "Maybe a mite high," Beeton said apologetically. "I think it got him in the ham."

Eggers shot three times, fast, and Nat looked reprovingly at him. After that he grew calmer, took better aim, and fired only when he had a good target. The townsman did not fire until the others had nearly emptied their carbines, then, while they were reloading, he caught an Indian running from one brush clump to another, and, with perfect aim, dumped the Apache midway, in a clearing. They all watched the man try to stand up. Each time he fell back to earth. Finally he began a painful scrawl toward cover.

Beeton was squinting along the northerly flank of the slope. Suddenly he touched Nat's arm and said, "Look there; it's the one you caught and tied up."

The Apache was running full tilt toward his friends, hands still bound behind his back. Nat shrugged. "Hold your fire," he said. "Let them get their wounded." It took a long time—the uninjured Indians were exceedingly cautious. They would not show themselves, and the only way Nat's friends knew when they were near an injured man was when the wounded Indian would begin to roll toward a particular clump of brush, or toward some big rock. "I think we've pretty well discouraged them from trying to get past to their friends."

"How many have we got?"

"By my count, three over here, and back along the rim, when their horses went down, another two."

"Five out of twelve. Not quite half."

Slim Eggers was lying motionless, his carbine resting between two dark rocks. He fired as Beeton stopped talking, levered, and fired again. Then he turned with a broad smile. "Makes it seven," he said. "Two more near where our prisoner went into the rocks."

"Will that discourage Rawgut?" the townsman asked.

"Well, it'll sure slow him down. He won't abandon his wounded."

"By God!" Beeton said, with a sharp outburst of breath. "There he is."

Rawgut was standing in plain sight, his gun in one

93

hand, staring up the slope toward the plateau. "Hold it," Nat said as Eggers crouched over his gun. "That's his defiance stance. Apaches only make that when they're whipped and want to die."

Eggers relaxed and all four of them watched the bandylegged, deep-chested Apache leader. "Maybe you could talk sense to him now," Eggers said. Nat shook his head.

"The first one of us to show himself will get shot. He wants to make us shoot him."

The Apache continued to stand in plain sight, as motionless as a lump of copper. "I'm sure itching to oblige him," Beeton said, but made no move to raise his gun.

"He's lost one man killed," Nat said, "only he thinks he's lost three. He's also got seven injured bucks on his hands, which means he can't attack and can't make a fast withdrawal. In other words, his raiding party has been a failure. As its leader he, also, is a failure. Rather than go back to San Carlos and endure shame, he wants to die here."

The townsman spoke slowly. "A person could almost feel sorry for the little devil."

"I'd feel a lot sorrier if I could get all his horses," Nat said. "Come on, let's head for the plain and see how Summer and Fritz are making out."

"You can't leave them here."

"Why not? Sure they're behind us, but there won't be much fight left in them. When we get around to it, we'll trail them."

They went back to the horses, mounted and rode south until the trail went off the plateau and down into Turner's Gap. The gloom of the canyon, with its attendant coolness, was good. Sounds of intermittent gunfire came to them, closer as they descended. Finally, hitting relatively level land, Nat led out in a reckless lope. As they approached the entrance to the canyon the sounds of battle grew louder still. Nat halted, raising his carbine as a signal for the others to stop. For a while he sought to determine, from the gunshots, where Summer's riders were, and where the Apaches were. Quite suddenly an Indian broke out of the underbrush near the canyon's mouth and came toward them as fast as he could run. He had a carbine in one hand and he kept twisting his head to look over his shoulder. A cowboy on a foam-flecked horse burst in sight whirling a lariat. The Apache dodged and twisted as the horseman raced close. The lariat sang through the air like a striking snake, settled over the Indian, and drew taut. Instantly the rider was on the ground going down the rope. The Indian cast his gun away and sought to gain enough slack to throw off the rope. Just before he succeeded, the Pine Tree man was on him. One terrific blow to the hostile's jaw felled him like a pole-axed steer. The cowboy bent, removed the rope, took up the Indian's carbine and levered it. Not until then did he smile—the gun was empty. He saw Nat coming toward him and for just a moment he grew tense, right hand dipping toward his hip-holster.

"Friends," Nat sang out, "that was pretty neat."

The rider relaxed and gazed down at his captive. "I couldn't figure out why the little cuss didn't shoot at me. His gun was empty."

"Where is Summer?"

"Down by the mouth of the canyon. He's got his hands full, too. There's thirty of them red cusses out there."

"Thirty!"

95

"Yep, we counted 'em as they come up. A few of 'em got into the rocks, but we managed to keep most of 'em out in the open. We must've gotten fifteen of their horses, too."

"Where's the Maltese Cross?"

"Danged if I know. The last time I seen John he was wonderin' the same thing. There's only twelve of us."

"Wasn't there another bunch of riders behind the Indians?"

"I never saw none, Sheriff," the cowboy replied, squatting to bind his prisoner. "Course, they on'y hit us a short while ago. Maybe them other fellers ain't got up here yet."

Nat looked at Beeton, who was suddenly busy examining the front sight of his carbine. "Either Fritz or Russ should be behind them," he said. "We saw two dustclouds." Beeton made no reply, booted his carbine and motioned ahead.

"We won't make no history sitting here. If there's just twelve Pine Treers and us, I expect we'd best push on."

Nat led them around the cowboy and toward the final fringe of hills beyond. The sounds of firing became flat and deadly. As they were dismounting John Summer came around a bend in the trail, afoot. He grounded his carbine with a hard movement and looked long at Nat. "Where's Maltese Cross? We can't keep 'em out of the canyon much longer."

"They were supposed to be right behind the Indians."

"Then they'd better get up here real quick. If they don't some of us'll be sleeping bald-headed tonight." Summer listened to the firing a moment, then turned back. Nat's voice halted him.

"Russ was supposed to come up behind Fritz. I know he turned 'em, or they wouldn't be here now."

Summer's face was dark as a thundercloud. "How many men's he got?"

"Seven, counting him."

"It wouldn't be enough anyway. We'll need at least twenty more."

"Have any of them got past you yet?"

"Not more than three or four strong-hearts. The rest are forted up behind their horses." Summer started forward again. "Come on, see for yourself."

As Nat was moving away Sheriff Beeton called to him.

"I'll take Slim and climb the slope," he said. "If any got past they'll be up in those rocks somewhere."

Nat gestured approval and went after John Summer. The afternoon sun bore down with a pitiless crush and the sky was a pale, faded blue.

CHAPTER 7

AS SOON AS HE WAS AMONG THE BRUSH AND ROCKS AT the canyon's entrance Nat could see why John Summer had been anxious. The Apaches, nearly all afoot, were using every shadow and every clump of brush to work their way toward the hills on both sides of the canyon's mouth. Many were almost close enough to risk the last dash to safety, and Summer's riders, lying close behind boulders, would then be flanked.

Westward there was nothing: no dun cloud of dust to indicate Russ and Ulen Fritz were hastening up, no moving objects which could be horsemen—nothing but sun-baked land as far as a man could see. Nat crouched beside a tall spire of rock and estimated the time: it had to be close to three o'clock. There would be another five hours of light, then the quick-falling summer night would obliterate everything, and the Apaches would be able to get behind them. He half turned at the sound of someone coming up. It was Summer, his face red and grimy with sweat. He dropped down beside Nat, raking the shimmering land with his eyes. "Maybe the man you sent to Ulen didn't get there," he said.

"That still doesn't account for Russ."

Summer's lips drew out thin. "The Indians could've gotten him."

Nat started to reply when Summer's hand sliced down hard against his arm. Nat twisted, flattening against the stone. Where Summer was looking an Indian appeared, advancing toward a dead juniper tree. Because of shadows, and brush and rock, it was difficult to catch the movement, but Nat had one glimpse. The Apache, moving doubled-up, was making for the far side of the spire Nat and Summer were crouched behind; he did not know white men were on the other side of the stone. Nat went prone, his chin in the dust, straining to see. The Indian disappeared in some brush, then reappeared, moving fast, in a sliding shuffle. When he was close, he made a half-turn, listened a moment, went swiftly forward. Nat gathered his legs under him, but John Summer was quicker. He sprang even as Nat was bunching his muscles. The Indian caught the movement from the corner of his eye, and spun around. Neither stepping back nor going for the knife at his side, he attempted to club with his carbine. He was too late. The blow did Summer no harm, and the white man was upon him.

Nat trotted forward, still crouched. The Apache was writhing in Summer's grip, arching his body, straining his legs, threshing left and right. Summer's face was a

98

beet-red blur, his arms desperately locked around the sweaty dark body. Nat swung his pistol, almost casually, and the little rustle of a limp body falling loosely on the flinty soil ended it. Summer gasped at the hot, thin air and a muscle in his neck twitched. "He was slithering out of my grip. Greasy as a snake." Nat used the Apache's headband to bind his wrists behind him, and stripped off the breechclout to make his ankles fast. "Be better to kill him," John Summer said, and, before Nat could reply, a swelling crescendo of gunfire up the slope behind them brought them both around.

"Injuns!" Summer shouted.

Nat caught his arm in a hard grip and pointed. "It's Maltese Cross!"

Summer's slitted eyes grew watchful. He said no more until a long line of cowboys, advancing afoot along the slope's upper reaches, came into view, moving downward towards the canyon's mouth. "How'd they get up there?" he asked.

"Darned if I know," Nat replied. "They were supposed to come up *behind* the Apaches. But that accounts for the long time it took them to get here."

"They rode back through the hills, circling behind us. Good thing they did. There's Ulen."

Nat started up the slope, dodging from rock to rock. John Summer followed, breathing heavily.

Big Ulen Fritz's chest was heaving with excitement when Nat and Summer dropped down beside him. He gave them a wide grin, and waved his pistol to the left and right. "We're all here," he cried, over the racket of gunfire.

"You were supposed to come up behind 'em."

"Hell, what kind of strategy is that? The idea was to keep 'em from getting to Rawgut's band. The best way to do that was to cut 'em off in front." Fritz made another large gesture with his hand-gun. "Look down there; if they'd seen us coming behind them they'd have rushed John's men." The wide grin became grim. "Now let 'em try it!"

Nat caught Fritz's arm. "Where's Russ?"

For a moment Fritz stared down where the Apaches were. Then he said, "He got shot, Nat."

"Shot?"

"Yeah. When I met your messenger we took the trail right away. Russ an' his boys were trailin' the Injuns— they were too close. The Apaches set up an ambush— you see, they saw Russ's dust—the kid rode right into it—him an' his men. Russ was out in front; they shot him and rode off like wild men. That's when I figured I'd take to the hills where I'd make no dust, and also so's I could get between them an' Rawgut, and maybe meet you and John."

"Shot bad?"

Fritz nodded, watching the fight below. "I had two of my boys go back to town with him on a litter. The rest of his crew is with me." Fritz got his legs under him as though to move down the slope with his advancing men. Nat caught hold of him. Fritz looked around, then shifted his attention to John Summer. The grin was gone. "I guess we'd better kill as many of them as we can," he said.

The three of them moved ahead to a shelter where they could see at all angles. Nat saw that the Apaches would soon be annihilated. The men up the slope could fire over their dead-horse barricades—and pick them off one at a time.

A loud wailing chant was rising from the Indians. They also sensed that the reinforcements had turned the battle's tide against them. One Indian scurried back a way and squatted in plain view, his head tilted back so he could look up into the ragged blue. He was motionless, as though waiting for the sky to tell him something.

Nat elbowed Ulen Fritz. "Call out your boys to cease firing. You too, John." Both ranchers obeyed, and the racket died gradually. Into its place came an eerie, unnaturally deep silence. Only two sounds lingered, the Apache chant, and the call of an injured white man for water.

Nat was moving toward an open space when a faint cloud of dust far out caught his attention. He pointed to it, and John Summer, eyes squinted, said, "That'll be those Texans." Until he spoke Nat had forgotten the drovers. His head jerked around. "They come down the canyon with their hands tied. We set 'em loose. They told us about Rawgut sneaking up and capturing them."

Summer watched the tiny dust banner a moment before continuing to speak. "I never figured them for cowards. Look at 'em go."

"They're heading for the herd."

Summer made a tight smile. "Maybe they're scared enough to point 'em south and keep going. I hope so, anyway."

Nat turned his attention to the Indians. They were lying still below a lifting, dirty-grey cloud of gunsmoke. He called out, and for a while there was no reply. Then the Apache who had walked back to pray got up, faced toward the canyon, and threw down his carbine. Nat started down the slope; Ulen Fritz called to him.

"We'll cover you."

The brush was thorny and the afternoon sun wilting hot. Nat ignored both. He did not feel that he had won a

101

victory. As he passed squatting cowboys, they spoke encouragingly. The Apaches did not arise from their barricades as he approached, and several gunbarrels tracked him. He stopped fifty feet from the nearest dead horse, unbuckled his shell-belt and let it fall. Around him dark, sweat-stained faces rose up. He ignored them until the thick-shouldered Apache leader came up; then he hooked his thumbs in his waistband and stood hip-shot, gazing at the warriors. "You rode into a trap," he told the Indian spokesman. "You have dead horses and injured men—but no dead warriors. It was planned to be this way."

"We have a dead warrior." The burly Indian jutted his chin toward a flat and lifeless body.

"One," Nat said.

The Indian raised his hand and bent down all the fingers. "More than one. Rawgut lost three by the river. He lost more beyond the canyon."

"No; near the river he lost one man. The other two are prisoners. In the canyon he has many hurt but none dead. There are no more than two dead, perhaps three. It is a small price for you to pay for starting a war."

"We rode only to help our relatives."

"And we rode only to prevent bad blood."

"We will go to Rawgut."

"No; you will go back to Gorman's Crossing with us."

"Why? So the *Pind-a-lick-a-ye* can hang us?"

Nat stared long at the Indian. "It should be clear to you that if we had wanted to kill you all, we could have done it just now. We will take you back as hostages—so other Apaches will not take up the hatchet."

"If we do not return our people will look for us."

"Let them look. We will be glad to have them see you

at Gorman's Crossing. They can see that we care for our prisoners well—so long as the other Apaches behave themselves."

"The soldiers will come, too. They will attack our people."

"Let the soldiers find your overdue beef allotment, if they feel like hunting."

"What else do you know?"

"Only what my old friend Rawgut told me," Nat replied. "Tell your men to throw their guns aside and move out into the open and wait."

The Indian turned slowly, looking at his companions. Those who had understood the drift of the conversation were hard-faced and defiant, the others sullen. Finally the Apache spokesman said, "I cannot order my warriors like the soldiers do. I am only a leader."

Nat turned and made a forward motion with one arm. The cowboys began streaming down the slopes of the canyon and out of its shadowed mouth. There were nearly thirty of them, and each man advanced with his gun held cocked and ready. The stillness rolled on endlessly. When Nat held his arm up a second time, the riders halted. Only two came up beside him—John Summer and Ulen Fritz. They stared hard at the group of Indians.

"Now tell them," Nat said. "They must either throw aside their guns and be driven back to town as prisoners, or they must use their guns. Tell them."

The spokesman turned, spoke gutturally, and fell silent. An Indian finally asked him in Apache where his gun was. The spokesman jutted his chin toward the weapon, far back where he had dropped it. An older warrior grunted and dropped his gun. Another older man followed his example. Then all the weapons fell, and Nat let his breath out slowly. "Get the horses," he said to John and Fritz. "Let's get back before dark, if we can."

It was a bone-weary crowd of horsemen that herded their cowed and sullen captives toward Gorman's Crossing. When they came onto the stage road they passed a startled freight train. The drivers and swampers watched them pass without a sound. Closer, Nat sent one of the Maltese Cross riders ahead to warn the citizens against congregating near the jailhouse, or making any hostile demonstrations. Then, as they were entering town, he had Summer make a phalanx of his riders, protecting the Apaches on both sides.

As it turned out, though, the townsmen were orderly. They were crowded five deep along the plankwalks, watching the strange procession, but they offered no interference. When Nat swung down, tied his mount and pushed inside the office, old Sheepy's mouth dropped down. He had been drowsing behind the desk. As the Indians filed inside his eyes widened. Finally, he shoved upright with one hand on his gun. Nat took the keys from their peg, kicked open the cell-block door, and motioned the Apaches past. They shuffled by, impassive and sullen, scarcely raising their eyes. When Nat had locked up the last one he returned to the office, hung the key-ring up, pushed back his hat and looked at John Summer.

"How many of your men were hurt?"

Summer jerked his head toward a rider with a scarlet rag around his hand. "One, shot through the hand."

"How about you, Ulen?"

"One man. I sent him back to the ranch. He had a broken leg."

The door burst open and George Semple scuttled in.

He looked from face to face until he found Nat. "What happened? Why did you bring them here? Their kinsmen'll tear the town apart. Have you sent for soldiers yet?"

Nat regarded the banker stoically, and turned his back. He poured a cup of coffee, and gestured for the others to help themselves. The room was thick with a scent of sage and sweat. The riders jostled Semple as they pushed toward the coffee pot. Still ignoring Semple, Nat said, "Sheepy, you better start hauling drinking water. Those Apaches've been out in the sun all day. They'll be able to drink ten gallons at least." The jailer's brows dropped down and drew together in a tufted glare, but he moved toward the water buckets obediently, without speaking. John Summer, watching his stamping exit, smiled.

"Mr. Summer," the banker bleated. "Mr. Fritz . . ."

John Summer eyed Semple distantly. "Missed you at the fight," he said. "I'd have given five thousand dollars to have had you out there, Semple."

"Do you realize what Hendrick's done by bringing those Indians to town?"

"I realize," Summer answered. "I realize something else, too. It never dawned on me until right this minute. You make me sick, Semple."

The banker's open mouth snapped closed. Color stained his face. Ulen Fritz turned around from over by the coffee pot. "You make me feel worse than that," he said in a deep-booming drawl. "You make me mad, mad enough to break somebody's back—yours, maybe."

"You're fools, all of you. The Apaches will come down here to set these men free. Can't you see that? Are you so ignorant you don't . . ."

"Whoa up there, friend," a tall, slab-thin cowboy said

105

from behind George Semple. "I never minded bein' called dirty, an' uncouth, an' primitive—all of which I've been called. But ignorant—now, Mister, I never liked being called that. Once, down in Sonora, I killed a man for callin' me ignorant. An' when it comes from a penny-roller, well, sir, I just plain got to step out an' take exception." A long arm reached out, fastened on Semple's collar, and turned him around. The cowboy's other hand held a wide-bladed knife. Semple made an inarticulate gurgle, and John Summer laughed aloud. Others laughed, even Nat smiled. "Now I reckon the wisest thing for you to do," the cowboy said, "would be to sort of apologize." The knife moved close and Semple gasped. "*Now!*"

"I apologize. I apologize to all of you."

"That's better. We accept," the cowboy said, sheathing his knife. "Now you got something to say, say it polite-like."

Semple's face, turned toward Nat, was pale and choked-looking. "Sheriff—good God, man—get troops down here as fast as you can. Please . . . Mr. Fritz, you're a reasonable man. Surely you know what the Apache reaction to this will be."

Fritz made no reply, and Nat said, "I know what it will be, Mr. Semple, and we'd sort of like to handle this without soldiers."

"But you can't, Sheriff. You know how many warriors are over at San Carlos!"

"I know. I also know it'll be a while before the other Indians figure out what happened to their friends. I mean to be the one to tell them."

"But you'd have to do that tonight."

"I mean to. Now if you'll go on home and leave this mess to those of us who've kept it from becoming a general Indian uprising so far, maybe we can get some work done."

Semple gazed at the faces a moment, and turned toward the door. As he was lifting the latch, Nat said, "And remember, Semple—no soldiers. Stay away from the telegraph office."

"All right."

After the banker was gone Sheriff Beeton, who had been sitting in silence upon the old couch, looked critically at Nat. "You don't mean you're goin' back out there tonight, do you?"

"Yep. just as soon as I see Russ for a minute."

Beeton looked at Eggers with a forlorn expression and shook his head. "Oh, lord," he said resignedly. "Well, come on. Don't just stand there holding that cup."

Nat started to speak, but Ulen Fritz interrupted him.

"How many men will you need?"

"I can't ask you to do any more, Ulen."

"Then I guess we'll all have to just sort of trail along."

Nat looked at Summer. The rancher's bloodshot eyes showed a twinkle of amusement through the weariness.

"He's right, Nat."

"You, John, and Ulen—Sheriff Beeton and Deputy Eggers. Five of us ought to be enough. We don't want to look like an army."

"The rest of you boys hang around town," John Summer said. "Just in case . . ."

Nat went to the door. "Grab something to eat. I'll be back in a little while."

He found Betty at Doctor Simpson's. Russ Bell was there, too, flat and gray. Simpson hooked Nat's arm before he entered the wounded man's room, and spoke in a brisk, lowered voice. "It's a bad wound, Nat. Through the body from front to back. But that's not what's letting him die. He just doesn't care about living. He's listless, indifferent—in a word, he's defeated. There comes a time in most men's lives when defeat is the easiest way out. If they're as sick as he is when they get that feeling, they usually die."

"Carrie Lee, Doc?"

Simpson inclined his head. "She's at Duncan. Betty wired over there. The stage came in well ahead of the Indian uprising, but the stage-line people won't let it proceed until they get word the roads are safe again."

"You mean she can't get back here?"

"Exactly."

"Does she know about Russ?"

"She knows. Betty asked the marshal over there to look her up at the hotel and tell her."

"We can't let him die, Doc."

Simpson leaned against the wall without taking his eyes off Nat's face. "I don't know how we can prevent it," he said. He straightened up. "Go talk to him now, but don't be long, Nat. He's weak, and his strength is failing."

Betty was sitting beside the bed holding one of Russ Bell's hands. Her eyes swept up as he came in. She did not speak. Nat knelt, squeezed her arm, and looked at the bloodless face on the pillow.

"It's me, Russ. It's Nat."

Bell's lids lifted, his dry eyes looked out. "Sure messed things up, didn't I, Nat? First Carrie Lee, then that killin', then I let the Apaches bushwhack me."

"The Apaches are all in jail—except Rawgut's band—and we're going after them now." Nat formed a lie in his throat. "Carrie Lee's on her way back, kid. She

108

. . . she changed her mind. She decided it was her fault—not yours." He felt Betty's eyes boring into his face. "She'll be here about dawn, Russ. You don't want to slide out without seeing her and the boy, do you?"

"Nat? Is that the truth?"

Nat got to his feet stiffly, stood looking down. "I'm not much of a liar, Russ, you know that."

The dry eyes lost some of their remoteness. "I'll be here, Nat. I'll wait."

"I'll come by as soon as I get back," Nat said, and walked softly to the door. Doctor Simpson looked around from where he was sitting at a table. He raised his eyebrows. Before Nat could speak a light hand brushed his arm.

"Can you work miracles, too?" Betty Aldridge said gently. "If he wasn't so dulled he'd know you've been in the mountains all day and couldn't have seen her."

"Would he know I couldn't have telegraphed her after I got back?"

"No, I guess he wouldn't know that—but I do."

"All right, I lied to him. Lying is like whisky, Betty, it was put on earth to be used sparingly—like I just used it—to save a man's life, maybe."

Doctor Simpson got up and crossed to where they were standing. "I don't know what this is all about, but I can guess," he said. "And I agree with Nat."

Betty took her hand away from Nat's arm. "I'm not arguing about it. I'm just thinking of the tragedy when he finds out it isn't so."

"He won't find out," Nat said. "At least I aim to try and fix it so that he won't."

"How?"

"By going on to Duncan when I'm through with the Indians; by seeing her, and sticking my nose in where it

109

doesn't belong."

"If you can do that," Betty said softly, "I'll believe you're a miracle-man."

He kissed her. Then he kissed her again. Doctor Simpson cleared his throat and held out his hand. "All the luck in the world, Sheriff. I think you're going to need it."

At the door Nat looked back at them. "It doesn't take luck to be a lawman, Doc, it just takes perseverance. You just keep plodding along—ask anyone in town, they can tell you that's all there is to it. Ask George Semple."

Doctor Simpson grunted as the door closed. "I wouldn't ask George Semple the time of day," he said.

Nat found Summer, Fritz, Beeton, and Eggers, waiting for him outside the office. They had fresh horses hitched at the rail. To the crowd of bystanders who were trying to start a conversation, Beeton and Eggers were indifferent. Fritz and Summer, who knew most of the townsmen, answered questions perfunctorily, and when Nat swung up they joined him with relief. As they were edging out into the roadway John Summer asked about Russ. Nat told him; he also told him about the lie. Summer fixed his gaze on the dark mountains and said, "If the horses hold out I guess we could make a sashay around by Duncan, on our way back."

Nat, believing Rawgut's band would be making its painful way back toward San Carlos, made for the Santa Clara. Where he crossed it the night-dappled water was speckled. "I smell cattle," Eggers said suddenly.

"Yeah. That'll be the Texans," John Summer replied. "They ought to be about two, three miles east by now."

They rode easterly, skirting the mountains until a

110

moon-limned pinnacle, jutting skyward in jagged solemnity, marked the end of the southerly range. There, Nat swung north until he found a well-defined trail. They traveled over this for an hour before they halted, and Nat asked Eggers to get down and study the trail for fresh tracks. Eggers reported there had been no easterly traffic for several days. Nat got down and began unsaddling. Beeton followed his example without speaking, but Ulen Fritz was less tractable. "Are we going to camp here?"

We're going to wait," Nat replied. "This is the trail down to San Carlos. If there are no fresh tracks heading east, it means Rawgut's band hasn't passed this way yet." He dumped his saddle, removed the bridle, hobbled his mount and sank down with a sigh. The black sky overhead was pierced by thousands of tiny pinpricks of light. Sheriff Beeton grunted down beside him, laid his head back against his saddle and said drowsily, "Slim's horse is fit to travel, Hendrick, so I expect we'll be leavin' tomorrow. I want you to know this sure has been an interestin' couple of days."

"I'll hate to see you go, Sheriff."

After a long silence, Beeton said, "Is Bell going to die?"

"I don't know. He's shot through."

"I kind of liked him. Slim did, too, an' Slim's like a puppy; when he likes a man there usually isn't too much wrong with him."

Ulen Fritz and John Summer came over, dragging their saddles. They eased down in silence and lay back, looking out toward the wide sweep of stars. Summer dug at a rock under his hips, unearthed it and pushed it aside. "When this is over I'm going to sleep for a week," he said.

Fritz's bass voice came back muted and drowsy. "No, you're not; you're going to start making up a drive. The Kansas City market's topping out high."

"Kansas City can go to hell."

"Maybe you'd rather sell old cull cows to the army at Fort Apache and lose money this year."

"I'd rather sleep for a week and let the army eat mutton," Summer said gruffly. He raised up on one elbow and looked over at Nat's big shadow. "Say, do you think Semple'll keep his word about not wiring the soldiers?"

"Right this minute I don't care what he does," Nat answered. "I'm too tired to care."

"If he does, that detachment at San Carlos will be the first ones to take the field."

"Hell," Ulen Fritz said in disgust, "they couldn't find their hip pockets with both hands, let alone any Apaches."

"But they could start rounding up Indians and scare half of them away from the reservation. That's what you were thinking when you told Semple not to wire 'em, wasn't it, Nat?"

"Yeah. It doesn't take much to make Apaches jump the line. I'd like to get this thing settled before it breaks into another Apache uprising. That's why we're out here tonight—instead of in bed, where decent folk ought to be."

Beeton pushed his hat back from over his eyes. "That's what lawmen are for boys, you know that. Ride day and night, fight Injuns, headwinds and high water, so's decent folks can sleep."

Ulen Fritz chuckled. The sound was cut off suddenly by the long fingers of Slim Eggers closing down around his arm. Fritz sat up quickly, peering at Eggers' profile.

In the softest of whispers he said, "What you hear, boy?"

"The trail. Someone's coming down the trail."

Nat shoved upright. "Slim, you and Sheriff Beeton watch our horses. Rawgut's men are mostly afoot. If they see our horses before we see them, they'll steal them." As the Nevadans moved off into the shadows Nat drew his carbine from its boot and motioned with it. Ulen and John followed him up the trail as far as a fringe of bull-pine, and there all three melted among the dark shadows.

The Apaches were coming slowly. There were two scouts out ahead, but they seemed more interested in the progress of the injured behind than in the dark night ahead. Nat gestured for his companions to use the butts of their carbines on the scouts. He covered them as they glided closer to the trail. After the Apaches had passed, both Fritz and Summer raised up and swung. The Indians fell without a sound. They were swiftly dragged into the shadows.

Nat could make out shapes, huddled and slow-moving. He was waiting for one in particular. When the main body of the band got abreast of Nat's tree, it stopped. The Apaches began to talk, some jutting their chins forward along the trail, others, listening to them, strained to see into the darkness. Nat guessed they had become alarmed over their scouts. As he watched, Rawgut came up along the column from the rear. The Indians clustered around him. He listened to them with his head moving from side to side, then he pushed past and started down the trail. Once he squatted, examining the ground. Nat moved, because he knew Rawgut would find the boot-marks made by Summer and Fritz.

He was almost clear of the shadows when Rawgut's

head came up, and he sprang erect, carbine thrust out ahead of him. Nat stopped without a word. The Apache was as still as the night, staring at him.

"Nan . . ."

"It's me, Rawgut, and I'm not alone. Shall we talk?"

The Apache lowered his gun and his shoulders slumped.

"We will talk," he said.

CHAPTER 8

RAWGUT'S BAND WAS BADLY SHOT UP. THEIR HORSES, six in number, were being used to transport the more seriously injured. When the whisper of white men ahead went down the line, the first impulse among the uninjured was to flee. When Rawgut called that they must remain still, lest they be shot by hidden whites, not a limb moved. As the spokesman and Nat squatted, Beeton and Eggers appeared with five horses. Fritz and Summer also came out of the shadows. The Indians behind their leader watched in stony silence.

"First," Nat said, "I am sorry for what I had to do. You must know I did not shoot to kill."

"I know. You shot to lame, to cripple, so that we could not run. You did your work well."

"I did not want to fight you."

"It is done. Where are the others—the ones I sent for?"

"In jail at Gorman's Crossing."

"So. And where are the yellowlegs?"

"Soldiers? There are none, Rawgut."

The Apache's smooth brow furrowed. "There are soldiers." He twisted half around and beckoned. A

114

young Indian came forward and talked briefly with his leader. Rawgut faced Nat again. "There are soldiers," he repeated. "This young man came to us from San Carlos. The soldiers were going among the people counting them."

"Then they knew your people were leaving the reservation," Nat replied.

"I do not wish to go back. They will put us all in jail."

"You knew that might happen when you left. You knew there would be punishment. The treaty says you must not leave San Carlos."

"The treaty does not say we must remain there and starve, and watch our children starve." Rawgut looked upwards for a moment, then he said, "Nan, we are old friends, but we are far apart. The night is black, the day is white—we are that far apart."

Nat got up, dusted his trousers and looked at the group of silent, motionless Indians. "What else did the young man say, Rawgut?"

"He said the people were afraid, that they were leaving the reservation and going to Mexico."

Nat saw Ulen Fritz and John Summer stiffen at the Apache's words. "By the desert trail below Duncan?" Nat asked. Rawgut nodded. "When they start?"

"When the young man came to us."

Nat looked at John Summer. "About two hours ago, I'd guess. What do you think, John?"

"We'll sure have to make tracks."

"Yeah. One more question, Rawgut. Did the women and children go, too?"

"Yes." Rawgut rose and studied the faces nearest him. He knew both Summer and Fritz. "Are you going after them?" John Summer nodded without answering. Rawgut looked at the ground. "The soldiers will be after them, too," he said, "and the patrols along the border—they will be after them. When I was younger the Apaches did not flee like deer from their enemies—in their own land."

Nat went to his horse, mounted, and looked down at Rawgut. "Times have changed," he said. "Maybe not for the better, Rawgut, but they have changed. You, more than the others, know that." He was silent a moment.

"Can you get your wounded back without help?"

"Yes."

"Then go back, and wait for us."

Rawgut lifted his head. "You try to help,"' he said, took something from his belt and tossed it to Nat. "For good luck."

Nat caught the object. It was the long dewlap from the butchered steer the Apaches had eaten in the canyon. He put it in a shirt pocket and spun away. The others loped down the trail after him.

Nat made no stop until the lights of Duncan lay on his right, twinkling yellow in the gloom. When the others came up Slim Eggers said, "Them cattle are around here somewhere, I can smell 'em."

"It'd be better if you could smell Apaches," Nat said. "I know the route they'll use, but they won't have any fires, so we'll have to go easy, or we'll overshoot them. We'll fan out, but don't get out of sight of the man next to you. If you run onto an Indian, let out a yell but *don't shoot*. No matter what the Apache does, *don't shoot*. All right?" The others assented, and Nat waited until they were spread out. Then he began a trotting advance across the rind of desert that grew softer, more sandy, as they progressed southerly.

Beyond midnight they halted at a seepage spring to

rest their animals. "Rawgut said the soldiers would be after 'em," Beeton said to Nat. "Did he mean they'd be behind 'em?"

"Well, if it's the detachment from the agency, they'll track them, yes. You see, there aren't more'n fifty troopers, and they won't try to close with the Indians until they've got reinforcements."

"Where'll reinforcements come from?"

"The border patrols. I reckon the soldiers will send a messenger out around the Apaches to find the patrols and alert them. That's the way it usually works. They try to get the Indians between them."

"I see. Will Apaches fight when they've got their women and kids along?"

"Yes, they abandon the kids and squaws because they know the soldiers won't harm them. Then the bucks make up war parties and try to slip around the soldiers into Mexico. After that—they raid and kill and plunder until hell won't have it."

"Well then," Beeton said imperturbably, "the thing for us to do is find 'em before the soldiers do. Right?"

"Right as rain."

Beeton made a quarter turn where he was squatting. "Show him, Slim."

Eggers pointed at the ground where he was sitting. Nat moved closer: there was a fresh moccasin track along the spongy earth near the spring. Eggers said, "Goin' west, Mr. Hendrick. I tracked him out a little, before you fellers got settled."

Nat sprang up. "Let's go. That track's not very old."

They changed course, riding south-westerly. The smoky moon was paling before Nat halted again and sent Eggers quartering for signs. John Summer looked at his stemwind watch and said, "Four o'clock, Nat. It'll start getting light pretty soon."

When Eggers came back he said there were no tracks. Nat knew they were finally ahead of the Indians. He thought a moment, then led out in a stiff-legged trot for a sagebrush fringe which lay between the desert's center and the big bend of the Santa Clara River. When they arrived among the covert a long, thin sliver of pale blue lay over the distant mountain peaks. "Let's cut brush," he said, dismounting and hacking at the tough sage with his pocket knife. The others, assuming he meant to make a signal-fire, followed his example. When they had a big pile of sage, Nat took down his lariat, tied four gnarled old clumps to it, then mounted his horse and dallied the rope around his saddlehorn. The other men watched him. Finally Ulen Fritz said, "What're you doin', Nat?"

"I'm recruiting a company of soldiers, Ulen. We'll ride across the desert in front of the Indians at spaced intervals, like soldiers ride. The Apaches will see the dustclouds and think the soldiers are between them and the border. They'll stop long enough to split up. While they're doing that, we'll ride hard and try to find them before they make their break."

In the first water-clear light of the new day Nat led out. Behind him, a quarter of a mile, came Sheriff Beeton. Behind Beeton another quarter of a mile, rode Ulen Fritz, trailed by John Summer and Slim Eggers.

Nat rode parallel to the border. The sage stirred up a great dust, visible for miles, as it slid along at the end of his lariat. He rode a full three miles, until he was satisfied the Indians had seen the dust. Then he drew up, shed the sage, and waited for his companions to join him. When the last man was up, Slim Eggers beat alkali dust from his clothing and spat cotton. "If I'd ever wanted to be a soljer," he said laconically, "this sure cured me. I bet I ate five pounds of dust."

Nat was mounting his horse when a far-distant diamond-flash of light caught his attention. He paused, leaning against his mount. "Heliograph signal over there at the base of the mountains. That'll be the soldiers from San Carlos signaling to us where they are."

Summer licked cracked lips and grinned. "We must've done a real good job, if we fooled them into thinkin' we're soldiers, too."

Nat finished mounting, just as Ulen Fritz said, "Look to the west there, a smoke signal."

It was a small, dingy burst of smoke rising from a sand-swell not more than two miles ahead. As they watched, two smaller spirals of smoke leapt skyward, one behind the other. Nat shortened his reins and started forward.

"Come on; we've got to get there before they split up."

They followed the deceptively smooth-appearing desert, rode down into long swales and over sharp outcrops of flinty stone. Sheriff Beeton urged his mount up beside Nat; over the clatter of hooves he said, "What'd they do that for? The soldiers'll know exactly where they are."

"They had to. The bands didn't all leave at the same time, and they didn't all take the same trail. They had to call them all together so they could make their plans." Nat looked over at Beeton's whisker-stubbled face. "Thank the stars they did, or we'd never have found them in time."

"Uh-huh. But if them soldiers aren't anxious to bust in on 'em, maybe we'd ought to speculate on it a little ourselves. There's only five of us, remember."

119

"Are you a praying man, Beeton?"

"Well, not exactly. Why?"

"Because maybe we'd better do a little praying about now. This is going to be the most dangerous part of what we're trying to do."

When they had covered a mile, two Apaches appeared out of a swale up ahead. They sat motionless watching the white men approach. When Nat raised his arm, palm outward, in the sign of peace, neither Indian responded. When they were closer still, Nat could see both Indians were stripped for war. He slewed to a halt, walked his horse the intervening distance, and drew up facing the impassive Indians. "Who is your spokesman?"

The Indians ignored him and studied his companions. One said, "Many leaders, many fighters. We did not ride here to talk. We came to fight."

"Fight soldiers," Nat said, pointing toward the mountains behind them. "And more soldiers," gesturing south.

The Indian pointed east and west. "The land is big," he said dourly.

"The land is changed," Nat fired back. "There are posses, cowboys, more soldiers. What happened to others will happen to you. Great leaders like Rawgut have been defeated. You too, will be hunted down." After an interval of stillness he repeated his earlier question. "Who is your spokesman? I want to talk to him."

"There has been too much talk, too much hunger."

The heliograph was winking again. Beeton, noticing it, touched Nat's arm and pointed. The Indians turned to look also. Finally, the silent one said, "This is Tawnay, our leader."

120

Nat watched the flashing light until it winked out, then he faced the grim Apache. "It is not too late. Apaches can slip around the soldiers and go back to San Carlos. It is the only way."

"Where is Rawgut?" Tawnay asked.

"At San Carlos."

"I do not believe you."

"I speak the truth. It was Rawgut who told us you were down here, heading for Mexico. We came here to turn you back. We waste time talking. You saw the soldier-dust along the border. You know more soldiers are behind you. Tawnay, for the sake of your people, you must go back. You must beat the soldiers back to the reservation."

"There is no food there."

"I will send you food."

"Others have said the same thing. We are still hungry."

"But this time *I* say it. My word is good. When you get back, ask Rawgut about Nan-tan Hendrick. Ask him if I lie."

"There is food in Mexico."

"There is death in Mexico. You know American soldiers can cross over the line. You know both Mexican and American soldiers will kill your people."

"But you will not," Tawnay said, with heavy sarcasm. "You are not the enemy of the Apache."

"I have never been his enemy. I am not his enemy now."

The silent warrior spoke briefly to Tawnay, and the chieftain looked bitterly at Nat. "We could not get back now," he said. "The soldiers are coming. Natchay sees their dust far back."

"I can fool the soldiers, too," Nat said. "If you will go

121

back I will cover your trail."

"How?"

"With dust. I will draw the soldiers after me while you escape. But you will have to be *coyote*, because all soldiers are not blind."

"Huh! An Apache child can disappear before soldiers."

"Then go, and go quickly. Split up and go out around them, Tawnay. Show the wiles of the coyote; show the wisdom of the Apache—but go fast."

"And this food—when will it come?"

"Within two days. You have my word."

The chieftain gazed steadily at Nat, until the sheriff thought he was going to sit there all morning. At last he lifted the single rein of his war bridle and spun his horse. "We will be at San Carlos tomorrow. If the food does not come by the day after, we will go into Mexico and no one will stop us."

Nat watched the Indians race away. The burning sun, hardly an hour high in the heavens, was making the desert a cauldron. He turned to his companions. "I thought it would take longer," he said. "I didn't expect to meet their leader first."

"It took long enough," Ulen Fritz said, mopping his reddening face. "Let's grab the brush and get to work."

They rode due west until the heliograph's winking showed less than three miles away. Then they dismounted, gathered sage, tied it to their lariats, and continued toward the soldiers. When they were close enough to see tiny moving objects, they turned south and rode at a long lope for a while, then swung west and kept going until the soldiers were in plain sight a half mile off, drawn away from the westerly passes back to San Carlos by the dustclouds. Finally, Nat halted his lathered horse, flicked the brush loose, coiled his lariat, and crossed his hands over the saddlehorn, watching the soldiers approach. John Summer dismounted, standing in the shade of his horse, and flung sweat off his face. "I hope they don't string us up."

Sheriff Beeton began making a cigarette. When it was going, the tendril of smoke spiraling up past his narrowed eyes, he turned to watch the thin line of approaching horsemen, riding spread out in skirmish order. "You know, boys," he said slowly, "I've been around Injuns all my life, but I'll be blessed if I ever helped any get away from the army before. Course, this desert air'll do funny things to a man." He removed the cigarette, licked its seam and popped it back into his mouth. "Look there—that one's a captain—an' he don't look pleased to see we're not Injuns."

The cavalrymen slowed to a walk, the officer out in front. Their faces, red and wet, showed surprise. The officer's brows were knit into a dark glare as he halted, staring at Nat. Without any preliminaries, he said, "I'm waiting for an explanation, Sheriff."

"Well, you could've been Indians, Captain, and if you were, by dragging brush we thought you might believe us to be a bigger force than we are."

The officer's expression did not change. His pale eyes bored into Nat. "You'll excuse me if I don't believe that, won't you? Now I want a straight answer, Sheriff. What are you doing out here?"

"Looking for Indians—like you're doing."

"And you found them—and you helped them ride around us—and for aiding and abetting an enemy of the United States you are subject to prosecution under Federal law."

"Did you see us with any Indians, Captain? Do you

123

have proof we aided or abetted anyone, Indians or anyone else?"

"I have circumstantial evidence," the soldier said, pointing toward the ground. "I have the tracks, showing where you rode and where the Apaches rode. I'm sure, when we back-track, we'll find where you met them. That will be enough."

Nat pushed sweat off his face with his sleeve. "I've got a little of that kind of evidence myself," he said. "Why did those Indians 'go out'?"

"Because they're Apaches—they don't need any other reason and you know it."

No, I don't. But I know starving people will do almost anything to keep alive. Why is their beef allotment overdue?"

"That's the Army's business," the captain said shortly.

"The hell it is," Ulen Fritz said. "Let me tell you something, sonny. I run five thousand head of cattle up by Gorman's Crossing. Every time you blue-bellies neglect to give the Indians their beef on time, they steal some of mine. That makes what they do my business. And another thing, when they jump the reservation, it's the settlers who pay—not the soldiers. Don't you ever forget that."

The officer's gaze froze on Fritz's face. John Summer spat, and looked toward the mountains. "You couldn't have turned them anyway. They would have wiped you out."

"No such thing," the captain retorted. "There is another column coming up from the border."

"Uh-huh," Summer countered. "That dustcloud you saw in company formation was us."

"What!"

124

"We did that on purpose, Captain. We wanted to turn those Indians back as badly as you did. We dragged brush to make those clouds you saw, and it worked. The Indians went back. Now listen," Summer's voice took on an affable, pleasant tone, "we were both working for the same thing, and we turned the trick, so why get all steamed up?"

The Captain slouched in his saddle. Great crescents of sweat showed at his armpits. "Did you see any cavalry down along the border." he asked. Nat shook his head without speaking. "I see. Well, we were certain those were five companies of cavalry. That's why we left the mountains and went down after the Indians."

"Good thing for you you didn't catch up with 'em," Sheriff Beeton said. "It would have been another Custer Massacree."

The captain looked down at Beeton without saying anything. Finally, he took off his hat, disclosed a bright bald spot, swiped at his forehead and replaced the hat. "You're Hendrick from Gorman's Crossing, aren't you? Yes, I thought I recognized you. I've heard you're quite a friend of the Apaches."

"Seems like they need friends now and then, Captain. Seems to me they could use some friends in the Army."

"They have them."

"Maybe not in the commissary department, though."

"The delay with the beef allotment is unavoidable, Sheriff Hendrick."

"That doesn't fill empty Apache bellies, Captain."

"Perhaps not, but they've got to learn to live as white people do. They've got to learn to be patient."

Nat's neck got red, but neither his voice nor expression changed. "There's no more patient people on the face of the earth than the Apaches, but they're not going to stand around and starve any more than you or I would."

The captain drew himself up. "Sheriff Hendrick," he said, speaking very clearly, "I don't think we'd ever see eye to eye where Indians are concerned, and I want to make it very clear to you that administering to the Apaches at San Carlos is not a civilian affair. Suppose we say that you cooperated with the Army today, in preventing the Indians from going down into Mexico for a raid, and let it go at that. Is that agreeable with you?"

"It is, but I'm bringing them some beef tomorrow, Captain, and I'd appreciate it if you'd stay out of the way when the drive gets up there."

"Why?"

"Because I want those people to know that at least *some* white men keep their word."

"You want to impress them with the fact that white civilians are more reliable than white soldiers."

Nat shrugged. "Interpret it any way you like, Captain, but there's only one way any of us can keep them from breaking out again, and that's by feeding them."

"And if I refuse to permit you to deliver the beef?"

John Summer whipped around with murder in his eyes. "You'd better not try," he said, in a stilled voice.

The officer looked into Summer's face and seemed to brace against the fury he saw. Without another word he turned his horse, barked an order, and led his troops back toward the mountains. The only sound, aside from the soft whisper of hooves striking sand, was Slim Eggers drinking noisily from his canteen. Ulen Fritz nudged his mount closer to Nat's side. "About this beef; I'll donate a hundred head."

"I don't think it's going to be necessary," Nat said.

"Let's head for Duncan and have a talk with those

Texans. They killed the first Apache, and they can make the first donation."

The ride back was through a land shimmering and writhing under the pale gold gush of sunblast. They did not arrive at the outskirts of Duncan until the first shadows were coming out, as long and thin as knifeblades. As soon as they rode into town, dusted white and wilted, people began congregating where they got down and tied up. Nat gave two lads a quarter to water and grain their horses, and tie them in the shade. He left the others at a saloon and made for the hotel. Finding Carrie Lee was no trouble; both she and Russ's son had been prostrated by the heat and were abed. Townsfolk had provided them with a fan, and damp rags hung over the hotel windows of their room. When Nat entered he felt the coolness soak in and relax his burning muscles.

Carrie Lee rolled her head on the pillow to look up at him. She seemed to have aged, but the darkness of her hair made a background for the loveliness of her face. She held out a hand. "Nat . . . oh, Nat!"

He sat on the edge of the bed and looked down at the baby. A scattered welter of small red dots were across his back. "Heat-rash," he said absently.

"But he's much better, Nat. He's been sleeping like that for an hour. The people have been wonderful, just wonderful."

"Most folks are, Carrie Lee, if you give 'em a chance to be."

"Tell me about Russ."

"Do you want to know about him?"

Her eyes misted over. There was anguish in their depths. "Nat, please don't hate me."

He took one of her hands and held it. "I don't, Carrie

127

Lee. I never could. How do you feel?"

"I feel all right," she touched her chest, "except in here."

"Feel good enough to travel?"

"Oh yes, Nat. Will you take me back? Please, Nat."

"I'm afraid I can't do that, but I'll fix it so that you can get back." He put her hand down on the sheet. "I didn't think you'd want to go back."

"I *do*. I never wanted anything so much in my life."

The tears were squeezed through her lashes. Nat took the hand again, and held it. "Carrie Lee, there's so much more to life than just you, or just me, or just Betty, or just Russ—or just your son. There's work and disappointment and sometimes a little happiness. It all works in together. It isn't all dances and ribbons." Her fingers closed around his palm with surprising strength. She said her husband's name, then repeated it. Nat disentangled his hand and stood up. Looking down, he thought how small , how frail she was. "Are you plumb sure you can travel back to Gorman's Crossing?"

"I could crawl there on my hands and knees."

"How about young Russ?"

"I'll take wet rags; he can make it, Nat. Please!"

"All right. You get dressed and meet me downstairs in fifteen minutes."

Outside the room the heat swept over him again. He did not notice it. In the hotel lobby two men got up at his approach. "Sheriff—Sheriff Hendrick. I'm Buel of the Great Western Stage Company. This is Mark Lawton. We heard from your friends that the Indians have gone back to San Carlos."

"That's right."

"Would you say it's perfectly safe for us to resume scheduled runs, then?"

128

Nat ran a hand along his scratchy jaw. "You wouldn't send the first stage down to Gorman's Crossing, would you?"

"One of the first would go there, yes."

"That's not good enough. A man's life depends upon the first stage getting there before noon."

"Impossible, Sheriff. It's eleven o'clock now."

"By two o'clock, then."

Mark Lawton's keen eyes bored past Nat's tired look. "A man's life depends upon it, you say?"

"That's right, my deputy. He was shot yesterday fighting Apaches. That's his wife and baby upstairs. If they don't reach him by two o'clock, I'm sure he'll die."

Lawton faced Buel. "That's not asking much for having the stages rolling again. I'll authorize it."

Buel's frown lightened begrudgingly. "All right, Sheriff. If you'll risk your deputy's wife and baby, I reckon the roads must be safe. We'll have the coach here in front of the hotel in ten minutes."

Nat went to the telegraph office and wired Doctor Simpson. When the reply came back that Russ was still alive and waiting, Nat sent a second telegram, paid for both, and went to the saloon where Beeton, Eggers, Summer, and Fritz were drinking beer set up by a large crowd of admiring Duncanites. At his entrance the crowd surged around him and bore him to the bar. Someone pushed a tepid glass of ale into his hand. He drank it, had a second one, then left them and went back outside with his companions trailing after.

Down by the hotel a little knot of women were talking and gesturing around Carrie Lee and the baby. Nat stood watching in the molten shade of the plankwalk's overhang. Moments later, when the stage came up and stopped, stirring up a cloud of acrid dust,

129

he saw Carrie Lee get in. As the stage moved past, gathering momentum, he held up his hand. Carrie Lee's tear-stained face, red from crying and from the heat, showed briefly. Then she was gone.

Sheriff Beeton spoke from behind Nat. "I thought I'd be heading south by this time, too, Hendrick. You got a way of makin' folks change their plans, haven't you?"

"Not her, Beeton. She had her mind all made up before we got here this morning."

"I'm glad of that, Hendrick, real glad. Young folks got lots of adjustment to make. Life ain't real easy."

"No, it isn't that," Nat said, turning. "Well, boys, we've got the Apaches turned back, an Indian uprising squelched, and Carrie Lee sent back to Russ."

"Got the damned army told off, too," Ulen Fritz said. "I'm still feeling good about that."

"Then suppose we hunt up those Texans and get Rawgut and Tawnay their doggoned cattle—then go home and sleep for a month."

CHAPTER 9

SHERIFF BEETON SIGHED WITH GREAT SADNESS WHEN they rode out of Duncan. The ale he had drunk caused perspiration to ooze out in a deluge. He rode slouched and loose in the saddle, his eyes closed and his jaw slack. Not until they got along the base of the mountains, westerly, and halted, did he come out of his lethargy.

Nat sent Slim Eggers up a crusty spire to see if he could locate the cattle. Eggers came down panting and sweatsoaked. "I didn't see 'em," he told Nat, "but I seen a lot of dust down along the river, and I figure it's got to be cattle, it's movin' so slow."

They continued on until the willows of the river afforded them some shade, and there big Ulen Fritz dismounted, tied his horse, put his valuables into his hat, and walked out into the water fully booted and clothed. He lay flat for a moment, then returned to his horse, shook off the excess water and wagged his head. "Pure bliss," he said. "Heaven couldn't be much better."

Nat dismounted, off-saddled, and led his animal into the water. As it drank he washed off its salt-encrusted back. Beeton and Summer followed his example, but Eggers hung back. "Ain't used to so much water," he explained. "An' I got a fear of drownin'." Nevertheless, he watered his horse, splashed water over his head, and joined the others in the shade of the willows. "We could rest a spell," he said to Nat. "Them cattle aren't movin' very fast."

Nat squinted at the sun, which was just about directly overhead. He looked at the others. Each face was whisker-stubbled, old and tired-looking. He lay back, drew his hat over his face, and slept. The others did the same.

They were awakened about two o'clock by the yapping of a coyote. After washing and drinking, they saddled up and struck off southerly again. Near a rolling landswell Nat caught the scent of cattle, and, when they topped out, the herd was visible a short distance ahead. John Summer smiled grimly. "They sure aren't wasting any time."

"No reason for 'em to; they haven't been exactly made to feel at home hereabouts," Nat said.

"I don't think they're going to take kindly to what you've got in mind, Nat."

"I wouldn't take kindly to it myself, but then I

131

wouldn't have shot that Indian until I was satisfied he was bronco, either."

They rode on, making a point of staying in plain sight. It was Slim Eggers, made wary by being shot at by the Texans, who called out that two riders were coming toward them. Nat watched the men a moment, and drew down to a halt. When the Texans came up both were balancing bared carbines across their laps. They did not seem relieved that the newcomers were not more Indians. Nat recognized them both, and sang out as they came up. "Where's Hays? We'd like a word with him."

"Then you got quite a ride ahead of you, Sheriff," one cowboy said, " 'cause he went up to Gorman's Crossing for a wagonload of vittles."

"When did he leave?"

"Mebbe two, three hours back. I don't expect you can catch him this side of town, but you'll find him there all right. Anything wrong?"

"Not a whole lot. Where do you aim to bed down?"

"A mile or two farther on."

Nat nodded and turned his horse. When he'd ridden a quarter of a mile Sheriff Beeton said, "Look back, Sheriff; them two haven't moved. Now, it ain't natural for a man to sit there in the sun like an Injun that long, is it?"

Nat looked back. The Texans were small in the distance, sitting where he'd left them. "They've got something on their minds, Mister Beeton."

"Like Indians, mebbe?"

"I wouldn't be surprised."

They rode down the long, blistering afternoon and pushed into Gorman's Crossing just before sunset. Nat let Eggers take his horse to the livery barn, went into his office and sank down behind the desk. The others found chairs and dropped down like stones. For a while no one spoke, then Beeton, stretched out on the couch, let out a long, full sigh. "With just a little bit of encouragement I could learn to ride one of these things 'stead of a horse, for the rest of my life. I'm about dogged out; how about you boys?" Fritz and Summer agreed. The door opened and Eggers came in. He jerked a thumb over his shoulder.

"He's down the road a ways. They're just beginnin' to load his wagon."

"Set down, boy," Beeton said to his deputy. "It makes my back ache just lookin' at you, standing up there."

Eggers went to the table in front of the gunrack and perched there. Of them all, he seemed the least used up. Finally he looked at Nat and said, "Want me to go down the walk and ask Hays to come up here for a minute?"

"I'd appreciate that, Slim," Nat replied, tossing his hat aside.

After Eggers left Ulen Fritz dipped water from a wooden bucket and drank deep. He sauntered over to the cell-block door and peered around it. "They're still here; I thought I could smell 'em. Indians smell like copper when they sweat. Hey, Nat, your jailer's asleep on the chair."

"Wake him up. We need more drinking water."

Fritz shook old Sheepy, who half-strangled on a bubbling snore and leapt up, blinking. Fritz jerked his head backwards. "Nat says we need more drinking water," he said with a wry smile.

Sheepy blinked faster, and went past Fritz into the outer office. When he saw Nat he began blinking harder than ever. "Hey," he chortled, "I'm sure glad to see you. There's been hell a-poppin' around here this afternoon."

133

"What kind of hell?"

"Well, sir, fust off, there were some fellers come here with George Semple. They had some kind of a paper f'turnin' the Injuns loose."

Nat looked up balefully. "But you didn't take it, did you?"

"Nosirree. You know ol' Sheepy better'n that. I told 'em to come back when you was here. Next, there was a half dozen army officers come in here lookin' for you."

"What'd they want?"

"You. They said you'd gone and helped Apaches break out of the reservation. They was mad as hornets, too."

"Where are they now?"

"Down at the saloon."

"All right; get us some water. I'll go down and palaver with 'em after a spell. Anything else?"

"Yeah. Carrie Lee come back on the Duncan stage. She's over at Doc Simpson's place with Russ right now."

"How is Russ?"

"I ain't seen him, but Doc was by couple hours ago. He said he was better'n he had any right to be."

The door opened and Will Hays, followed by Slim Eggers, came into the office. He was wearing his mirthless smile. Before Nat could speak he said, "By golly, Sheriff, I never got a chance to thank you for savin' our bacon from them cussed Apaches. We're sure beholden to you."

"Maybe you won't be after you hear what I have to say." Nat pushed upright in the chair, gazing at the Texan.

"Hays, you started this mess by killing that Apache."

"What'd you expect us to do, let him run off our

134

critters and fetch his friends back to lift our hair?"

"Well, the fact is, you've got to give them a hundred head of your cattle in payment."

Hays' face went blank. His eyes didn't waver from a long study of Nat's features. Finally he spoke. "Oh no, Sheriff. I ain't givin' them Injuns nothing—unless it's bullets. They attacked us, we didn't attack them."

"You attacked them when you killed that buck. You put every man, woman, and child in this area in jeopardy, when you did that. You almost started a war, and only a lot of co-operation and hard riding prevented it. Now, the least you can do is help us keep those Indians pacified by giving them cattle for the Indian you killed."

Hays looked at the faces around the room. "You got no legal right to do this, Sheriff, and I don't feel like I owe them Injuns anything."

"How about the men who saved your lives yesterday afternoon? Don't you think you owe them something?"

"Shucks, Sheriff, I'll buy 'em all a keg of whisky. Down in Texas that's what we do when a body does us a good turn. But givin' away a hundred of my critters—no; I can't see my way clear to do that—not even if it means another Injun war."

"Then how many head will you give?"

Ulen Fritz got up stiffly. He towered over Hays and his expression was unpleasant. "Come on, Texan; whatever you say I'll double. I'll tell you one thing, though, you're going to give some cattle, or we're goin' to ride out there and stampede 'em. The Indians'll get more'n than a hundred head if we drive 'em down the San Carlos trail."

"Well, sir," Hays said, gazing brightly at the uncompromising faces in the room. "You boys ride out

135

to my camp, and we'll decide just how many I'll give— but it ain't going to be any one-fourth of my herd, I'll tell you that."

Sheriff Beeton groaned. "Ride down there again? Why don't you just drive the critters up here to us?"

"No, I want you all there to he'p me pick 'em out. That sure ain't askin' too much, when a man's giving away cattle, is it?"

Nat put his palm flat on the desk and pushed upright. "All right, I'll be along in the morning. You keep the cattle at the bedding ground until I get there."

"Sure, Sheriff," Hays said. "I'll be waitin' for you."

After the Texan was gone, Sheriff Beeton got up and ambled to the door. "Slim and me're going to get some sleep. See you in the mornin' before we head south, Sheriff." He left, with Eggers moving behind like his shadow.

Nat watched Sheepy enter the office with two buckets of water, and disappear beyond the cell-block door. He looked over at Summers and Ulen Fritz. "Go on home, fellers, and thanks. I'm not very good with platitudes, but I've got a long memory. I won't forget the help you gave me."

When he was alone in the office, Nat lay down on the sofa and fell asleep almost instantly. He did not awaken until Sheepy had him by the shoulder, shaking. He opened his eyes and sat up.

Three army officers were standing across the room by his desk. He nodded to them, went to the basin, splashed water against his face, and faced around. "What can I do for you gentlemen?"

The eldest of the three, who wore a major's insignia, said, "I'm John Eaton from Fort Apache. We've heard you were instrumental in keeping the San Carlos

Apaches from getting into Mexico."

"Yes, I was; so were a lot of other men."

"I'm on an inspection tour of the Territory, Sheriff, and I wanted to stop by and tell you how much the Army appreciates what you've done."

Nat looked at Sheepy, who was scowling in a perplexed way.

He looked back at Major Eaton. "I thought you had something a lot different to say. In fact . . ."

"Well, as a matter of fact," the major said in an apologetic tone, "until I'd heard the stories around town here, I'd been led to believe you'd had a hand in something altogether different. Knowing different, now, I didn't want to ride on to San Carlos to complete my inspection tour until I'd shaken your hand."

Nat felt his hand being pumped. He looked beyond the major at Sheepy again. The old man rolled his eyes, shrugged resignedly, and lugged the buckets of water out of sight. When the major dropped his hand, Nat said, "Major, there's a favor you could do me at San Carlos. In fact, there are two."

"Name them, Sheriff. Just you name them."

"Well, first off, you could find the young captain who commanded the detail from San Carlos this morning, and whom I met down near the border, and explain to him that a little more talk and a lot less shooting will make friends of the Apaches a heap quicker."

"You have my word, Sheriff; it shall be done."

"And the other thing, Major. There are two Apache spokesmen at San Carlos. One is called Rawgut, the other is known at Tawnay. You could tell them that I will be up there with their cattle tomorrow, and if they'll meet me at the base of the mountains it'll save a heap of riding."

137

"I'll do it. Anything else, Sheriff?"

"Well, if you have the time, maybe you could find out what's delayed the beef allotment. It was because of this delay that we nearly had an Indian war."

"You mean the Indians haven't been fed lately?"

"They not only haven't been fed, sir, but those cattle I'm wheedling off a Texas herd will be all they'll have to eat until their regular allotment gets to the reservation. If it doesn't get there pretty soon, they'll have eaten up all the critters I bring, and they'll be hungry again. And, Major, hungry Apaches are about the most savage critters on earth."

"Sheriff, you can believe me when I say I'll find out what's wrong up there. That's part of my job, sir."

"Thanks, Major, and good luck."

"Thank *you*, Sheriff."

Sheepy came from the Apache cells with his empty buckets. He watched the last officer close the door, and he put the buckets down, hard. "Now, what in tarnation made such a change in that rooster? When he was in here this afternoon he was fit to be tied."

"Does he get pretty mad?" Nat asked, picking up his hat.

"Mad? Why, he gets redder'n a beet and he shouts like a bull-buffalo."

"That's good. Maybe he'll get mad at San Carlos."

"Where you goin'?"

"Over to see Russ."

"Well, what about these prisoners? They're about to drink the well dry."

"Then feed 'em," Nat said, and went out into the soft, pale night.

He heard his name called softly as he was turning toward the roadway. It was Betty Aldridge. She swept

138

up with a big smile, and hugged him. "For a miracle-man you look terrible."

"I don't suppose I smell like perfume either. What time did Carrie Lee get back?"

"A little after two o'clock. She looked tired but happy."

"And Russ junior?"

"He was just plain mad." She took his arm and started across the road with him. When they were on the plankwalk on the far side, where the shadows were deepest, she said, "Are you hungry?"

"Hungry? Me? Why, just barely enough to chew the kicking end of a wild horse, that's all."

"And would you like a steak with onions, a gallon of coffee and some chocolate pie?"

He halted and pulled back. "You're trying to trap me into saying 'yes'. Well, you win. I'll marry you—but you've got to feed me like that every night."

"And every day, too. Kiss me, Nat."

Moments later they were walking toward Doctor Simpson's house again. When he stopped to draw back the gate she said, "No . . ."

"No what?"

"No—you don't smell like perfume."

Doctor Simpson greeted them with a warm smile and a hard handclasp. "Nat, you've sent the best medicine. I think he'll make it. Of course it's going to be a long time before he can be up and around."

"Sure. Can we see him?"

"Them," Simpson said, with emphasis. "He's still got his 'medicine' in there with him."

Betty opened the door softly, and Nat followed her into the room. An odor of medicinal, particularly carbolic acid, was strong in the air. Carrie Lee looked up at them from a rocking-chair beside Russ's bed. She made a small smile. "Russ, Nat and Betty are here." The wounded man turned his head and looked up.

"Nat, you need a shave about as bad as I do."

Nat dropped down on the edge of the bed. "Glad you noticed. Feeling any better?"

"A lot better."

"Where's junior?"

"Sleeping in Doctor Simpson's parlor."

"I envy him."

"Carrie Lee told me the Indians are back at San Carlos."

"Yeah, they're back. Beeton, Eggers, Summer, Fritz, and I caught 'em down by the border and talked 'em into going back. Tomorrow I'm going to take some cattle up to them."

"Whose cattle?"

"Those Texans'. They started the fight by killing that buck. They can pay off part of the debt by giving a few head."

"Have Beeton and Eggers left yet?"

"No. They're pulling out in the morning." Nat's dulled eyes shone briefly. "I'll bet they never come down around this part of Arizona again."

Russ smiled. "I'd sure like to see them before they go."

"I'll tell them."

Betty said, "No, you won't. You'll go get a bath and some sleep. I'll tell them." She tugged Nat gently off the bed. "He'll be around tomorrow, Russ; right now he's dead on his feet."

Russ's grip was firm on Nat's hand. "I sure learned a lot this past week," he said.

Nat gazed at Carrie Lee and nodded. "I reckon we all

140

have, Russ. See you some time tomorrow."

When they were back outside Betty led him to the café. The first edges of darkness were crimped around the distant mountains and shadows lurked in the room. When the lamp was lit a voice came from a chair by the window. "By grannies, it's about time you showed up. Them cussed prisoners of mine are . . . . Well, hullo, Nat."

"Sheepy!"

"I'd sure admire if you wouldn't interfere with the feeding of the prisoners," Sheepy said. "That there Duncan highwayman's taught them blasted Indians how to rattle cups on the bars. It's enough to drive a man to dipping snuff."

Betty said, "They can all wait, Sheepy. Nat comes first."

Sheepy watched owl-eyed as Betty fed Nat an enormous steak, four cups of coffee, three helpings of potatoes, and two pieces of chocolate pie. When the sheriff was leaning back to make a cigarette, Sheepy groaned aloud. "You'll founder him, Betty. He's proba'ly founded right now. I heard of killin' men with kindness, but this is the first time I ever seen it."

"Help me with these pans," Betty said. After Sheepy had trudged out of the café laden with food, she took off her apron and shook out her hair. The sturdy look of her, and the long, frank glance she bent on him, made Nat's weariness fall away. "How about you and me huntin' up a dance?" he said.

"You're going to the hotel, take a bath, and sleep until sun-up. Now go on."

"Tomorrow night?"

"Tomorrow night you're going to do the same thing. Maybe the night after, though."

He got up and went as far as the door. "You know, I reckon I'll marry you tomorrow night," he said. "Then go to the dance the next night."

He ached with weariness, but inwardly he had a sense of well-being. After he'd bathed, he lay on his bed under the lowering roof, and let heat and stillness envelope him. He slept like a log, too, but habit awakened him at sun-up. Refreshed, and with the dawn-scent strong in the air, he dressed and went downstairs to the café, ate a big breakfast and walked out onto the plankwalk.

Gorman's Crossing was beginning to stir. A man he recognized as a nester from beyond town left a crate of eggs at Betty Aldridge's café, and opposite two cowboys were washing at the livery barn trough. He sauntered down to the jailhouse and entered. Sheepy was sleeping on the horsehair couch. He had a paper over his face and his snores made it flutter a little. Hearing Nat come in, he half strangled on a snore, snatched irritably at the paper and sat up.

"Time to feed your prisoners," Nat said.

Sheepy explored the inside of his mouth with his tongue, and ran crooked fingers through his thin hair. He got up and began stuffing his shirt into his trousers. "Why don't you turn 'em loose? You're goin' to have to sooner or later anyway, they're the Army's responsibility."

"I'll have the Army come by and pick them up today, but meantime they've got to be fed."

"What about the Duncan hold-up?"

"We'll hold him for the circuit judge. He'll be along in another week or ten days."

Sheepy went to the wash basin and filled it with water.

"Them two Nevadans was in here an hour or so back."

"They got an early start, huh?"

"Early enough to wake me out of a sound sleep," Sheepy spluttered from behind cold water. "They said to tell you they'd be over at the livery barn."

Nat scowled at the old man's back. He crossed to the livery barn, and entered the wide, ammonia-scented alleyway. Waiting on a buggy seat, legs thrust out and shoulders slouched, were Beeton and Eggers. The older man turned his head as Nat came up, and said, "By golly, you sure had a long sleep."

"I thought you fellers would be five miles out by now."

"Well, you know, Sheriff," Beeton said drawlingly, "me and Slim got to talkin' last night, and we concluded that we might as well hang around an' see the last dog hung."

"What do you mean? We got the Apaches corralled, and Russ's going to make it. What else is there?"

"Them Texas cattle, Sheriff. When Hays was talkin' to you yesterday, we sort of got the impression he didn't want to give you no cattle."

"But you saw how he changed his mind."

"Mebbe. Anyway, Slim and me figured we'd ride out there with you today."

Nat squinted at Beeton. "You think he'll go back on his word?"

Beeton got up and jerked his head at Eggers. The deputy went to a pair of tie-stalls and came back leading saddled horses. "I don't know whether he will or not," Beeton opined, but I've always sort of prided myself on being a pretty fair judge of men, and it's sort of stuck in my craw whether I'm right or wrong about Hays."

143

Beeton took his reins and grunted up into the saddle. He faced Nat again. "If we didn't go out there with you today, we'd always wonder whether you got the critters or not." He smiled.

Nat laughed. "By golly, Beeton, you're one for the book. Well, I'll sure be happy to have you boys ride with me again. Fact is, I'm getting sort of fond of you. just a minute, I'll get my horse."

They left Gorman's Crossing and rode in silence for some distance. At length Nat twisted in the saddle to look at Beeton. "I owe you a lot," he said. "Maybe I can get leave of absence and help you hunt down your gold rustlers."

"I'll find 'em, don't fret about that," Beeton replied. "Anyway, I don't think these folks could spare you. You know, Sheriff, for such an out-of-the-way place, your county's sure got its share of short fuses." Beeton watched his horse's lop-ears bob back and forth as the animal trudged along. "And I got to wonderin' yesterday if they appreciated all you do for 'em. Now you take that fat little banker . . ."

"Semple? He's all right, Beeton. He just gets roiled up real easy."

"Mebbe. I don't think he understands yet that you kept his damned town from bein' attacked. After we left you yesterday we went down to the saloon for a few ales, and there he was, talkin' a blue streak to some Army officers. He had 'em all fired up, too, until Summer and Fritz come in."

"Then what happened?"

Beeton smiled softly in recollection. "It was about like watchin' ice water hit a fan behind a lot of sleepin' cowboys. That Fritz feller's got a voice like a stud-horse anyway. He called Semple just about everything he

144

could think of, grabbed him by the britches and threw him out the doors, then him and Summer laid it on the line to the Army. You never seen expressions change like them soljers' faces did. When Summer and Fritz was through, you could of heard a fly walkin' in that saloon. The soljers thanked 'em and walked out of there as stiff-legged as could be. Now, the point I'm makin' is that these folks don't know what a good man they got for a sheriff."

"They re-elected me last term."

"Yeah, then they tried to shoot you and Russ when Russ gunned that outlaw."

"You know how folks are, Beeton."

"Sure I do. That's why I'm sayin' they don't appreciate what you done for 'em. Now, up in Cedar County, we'd have give you a medal and a raise in pay. Cedar County's pretty savvy about men, and we always need your kind up there. The pay for a first-class deputy's . . ."

Nat's laughter interrupted the Nevadan. "Cedar County's the lucky one," Nat said, his laughter subsiding. "You're as sly as they come, Beeton."

The Nevadan looked at Nat with a ghost of a grin. "Well, you can't blame a man for tryin', Sheriff. I'm always on the watch for good men for deputies." He looped his reins and began worrying up a cigarette. When it was going he exhaled mightily and spoke again. "If you ever do decide to take a change of scenery, Hendrick, look me up."

"I will."

They cut the Texan's trail five miles south of Duncan at the Santa Clara, splashed across it and kept going. The sun was riding loose and easy overhead, and the sky was taking on its pale, faded hue. Nat searched the horizon for clouds, found none, and said, "I guess that thunder shower blew over." Beeton nodded without speaking and Slim Eggers, watching the ground, began to frown. He said nothing for another mile, then he drew up, pointing.

"See them fresh-chewed willows? That's where the herd camped last night. Look at the stalks; they haven't begun to mottle up from the sun yet."

Nat and Beeton studied the willows, then turned their attention to the ground. "I think he's right," Nat said, finally. "Hays didn't wait like he said he would."

"I never expected him to," Beeton growled. "Come on; they can't be more'n a mile or two ahead."

They followed along the river in the wake of the Texas herd, and the scent of cattle was strong in the air. Where the land rose in a long roll, and dropped down, Eggers urged his horse ahead, as keen as a terrier on a trail. Both Beeton and Nat saw him rein up sharply and sit motionless atop the roll of land. Beeton kneed his mount and Nat, sensing trouble, was turning in the saddle when a voice, even and very hard, hit him in the back.

"Sit still. Don't make a sound."

The Texan had been among the willows. Nat saw him moving forward now, carbine in both hands. He knew him as soon as he heard the voice: Hays' companion the night the owl's eye had been shot out at the Durelle Saloon back in town.

"Never mind about your friends. There's a feller up there to take care of them." The Texan jerked his gun sideways. "Now then, you just ride up there with 'em, and keep both hands in plain sight."

Nat let his horse walk slowly toward Beeton and Eggers. Until he was traveling along the landswell's lip he didn't see the other Texan. He let his mount stop when it was beside Beeton. Anger burned bright within and some of it showed in his eyes. "What the hell do you think you're doing?" he demanded of the Texan in front of them. The man's long lip lifted in a broad grin when he replied.

"Well , sir, we just didn't know who you was, when we seen you ridin' down this way, and we figured to sort of make sure you wasn't no Injuns or other vermin."

"Now you know who we are, and you can put that gun down."

"We know," the Texan said, "but Sheriff, Will told us not to trust nobody hereabouts and we ain't goin' to. What d'you want down here anyway?"

"I want to talk to Hays."

"What about?"

"That's between Hays and me."

The Texan grounded his carbine and stood slack, looking up at the mounted men. His face was thin, weasel-like, and weathered to the color of saddle-skirting. There was a thin edge of blood-lust in his glance, and it never wavered. Finally, without removing his eyes from Nat's face, the Texan spoke to the man behind them. "Fetch Will; he'll want to see what we got." As the second Texan headed back for the willows and his saddlehorse, the first took a twist of molasses-cured chewing tobacco from his pocket, bit off a corner and pouched it in his cheek. He smiled again. "You know, fellers, I'm beholden to you fer gettin' us clear of them Injuns. I figured for a while we was all a goner." The steady eyes went from face to face. "Us boys knows Comanches pretty well, but we never had no run-ins with Apaches before. But we learnt, boys, we learnt.

147

The next time I see an Apache he'll be as good as dead. Fact is, if we wasn't in a hurry with these critters we'd go back to them mountains and collect us a bounty-full of Apache topknots; there's one thing them Apaches ain't been taught yet—you don't go pushin' us Texas boys around and live long t'tell about it." The cowboy's eyes suddenly widened and froze on Nat's shirt-front. His nasal voice trailed off into silence for a moment, then he said, "What's that hairy thing you got in your pocket there, Sheriff?"

Nat looked down, and remembered Rawgut giving him the dewlap for good luck. "It's the road mark off one of your cattle."

"Let me see it."

Nat removed the dewlap and tossed it down. The Texan caught it, hefted it, and looked at it closely. "Where'd you get it?"

"An Indian gave it to me. They evidently butchered one of your critters up the canyon somewhere."

The Texan rolled the dewlap in his palm, studying it. He looked critically from Nat to Beeton, to Eggers, and back to Nat again. "I guess Will'll want to know about that." The sound of riders coming made the cowboy turn. Without looking back around he said, "Here's Will now."

Hays was riding a leggy grulla ridgling with a big crested neck and a wavy mane. He reined up, nodded shortly, and was going to speak when the Texan on the ground held up the dewlap. "Here; an Injun give it to the Gorman's Crossing lawman."

Hays snatched at the dewlap, examined it closely, and looked up. Nat was surprised at the hardness of his face.

"How come an Injun to give you this, Sheriff?"

"As a good luck omen. Listen, Hays; you told me

yesterday you'd wait in camp for us to come and get the cattle for the Indians."

Hays stared at Nat without answering. He pocketed the dewlap and his expression relaxed. When he spoke he sounded natural again. "You know how it is, Sheriff; a man's got to keep his critters movin' this time of year. There ain't much for 'em to eat at the best."

"I guess we can let that pass, but this business of sneaking up on riders and getting the drop on them's a little unusual in this part of the country."

Hays' cold, pale eyes crinkled into an apologetic grin. "By golly, after what happened to us with them Injuns of yours, we're just naturally a mite leary."

Beeton interrupted. "I've seen you somewhere before, Mister. Ever been in Northern Nevada?"

"I've been up there," Hays said simply. "Bought cattle there from time to time. Ain't been up there lately, though." He looked briefly at Eggers, then returned his attention to Nat. "About them critters for the Injuns, Sheriff. I'll give you money to buy a hundred head from hereabouts. Maybe from that feller Summer, who got all upset when we used his gatherin'-ground."

"That would take too much time, Hays. I promised the Indians we'd have cattle at San Carlos no later than today. We can cut out a hundred head right here, drive them around the base of the mountains and be at San Carlos by early afternoon."

Hays' affability vanished gradually as he stared at Nat. "Not these cattle," lie said quietly. "I don't have any critters I want to part with."

"I don't think you've got much choice, Hays."

The Texan leaned forward in his saddle, then settled back again. Turning to the man beside him, he said, "Go get the boys; if we've got to do some cuttin' we'll need

149

the whole crew." While awaiting the return of his messenger and the rest of his trail crew, Hays talked about the hard drive he'd had. Sheriff Beeton finally scratched his head and interrupted.

"You told Sheriff Hendrick you drove your herd east along the Blackfoot River, ain't that right?"

"Sure is, mister."

"You must've had quite a time doing that."

"Naw, it wasn't very hard," Hays said. He stopped suddenly, looking closely at Beeton. "What're you aimin' at, Sheriff?"

"The Blackfoot river don't run east and west, Hays, it runs north and south."

The Texan's face darkened with blood, and his eyes narrowed. "You callin' me a liar, lawman?"

Beeton shrugged. "If the boot fits, wear it," he said. "Only you could've been crossed up in your directions."

Hays remained motionless for a long time, looking at Beeton. Finally, with the sound of his riders sweeping up, he reached down with no speed, drew his hand-gun and cocked it. "You fellers been hazin' me long enough," he said flatly. "Now turn them horses around and ride back where you come from, and don't come back. If you do, you'll get the same dose that cussed Injun got. *Now git!*"

"Hays . . .!"

"Rope it, Hendrick! I got nothin' more to say to you. I offered to buy cattle for your doggoned redskins, and you turned me down. I got to do no more. Now get to ridin' and remember what I said about comin' back."

Beeton turned his horse and started back the way he had come. Slim followed after him. The last one to turn away was Nat. He followed the others north along the river until they were hidden from view of the Texans,

150

then he halted and called to Beeton. "I reckon you were right, Sheriff. I don't think he ever meant to give us any cattle."

"It ain't losin' the cattle that's got my dander up, Hendrick; it's the way he run us off."

"He didn't run us off, and he's going to give us those cattle, too."

"How do you figure to work it?"

"Come on; we'll go out around 'em, and where they have to ford the river again, about a mile south, we'll cut out the first hundred across and drive 'em off."

"But you got to have a writ to do that."

"I'll get the writ later. Where the river makes its bend is the line of my jurisdiction. If they get across I can't touch them."

"By golly, I'll bet Hays knows that. I'll bet he found that out up at Duncan."

"Probably. Let's go."

They rode hard and didn't draw rein until Nat waved his arm south-easterly. They halted only long enough for him to explain that the river's turn lay in that direction. Another hour's hard riding brought them within sight of the willows. Nat abruptly changed course again, heading farther south. As he was splashing across the river, Beeton came up close. "I seen him, too," he said. "Hays is a long way from being stupid, puttin' a guard there to watch for us."

Nat left his horse with Slim Eggers, Beeton did the same, and began slipping up through the rank growth of willows toward where he had seen the dozing Texan at the crossing. Capturing the man wasn't difficult, but silencing his profanity after they'd tied him was; Beeton solved it by bludgeoning the captive into insensibility. Beeton continued to kneel beside the unconscious form.

151

When Nat said it was time to return for their horses, the Nevadan pointed at the Texan. "At a distance I could pass for him." He tossed his hat aside and donned the Texan's headgear. It fitted. Beeton stood up. "You fetch Slim and keep out of sight. I'll sit this feller's horse until they come up, then I'll wave 'em on across and ride point so's none of 'em'll get a good look at me. When there's enough across, you boys bust in, cut the herd in two, and drive 'em north as hard as they can run."

Nat went back and got Eggers. They both hid in the willows until they saw Beeton flag his arm at the approaching Texans, who waved back, bunched the cattle and drove them into the river. When what looked to Nat to be a hundred head were on the far side, he and Slim burst from the willows, driving hard toward the herd. They yelled and the cattle nearest them broke into a wild charge. Soon all the cattle across the river were stampeding northward, while the animals in the water and on the far bank, began bawling and milling.

Will Hays appeared briefly at the crossing. He yelled at his men, and they plunged into the river in pursuit. Because the water was choked with panicky animals, they did not clear the near bank until the three lawmen had their part of the herd a half mile away and running hard. Hays' grulla ridgling, more powerful than a stud-horse, soon out-distanced his companions' mounts. The Texan rode erect with his carbine in one hand. He fired twice, but the range was too long.

When Beeton fell back where Nat and Slim were, his face was red with excitement. He jerked a thumb backwards and yelled over the bawling thunder of running cattle. "It's Hays; he's coming up fast." Nat made no reply, and the three of them concentrated on heading the stampeding cattle toward the base of the mountains. A stifling dustcloud rose high into the air, and Slim coughed and swore as he faced into it.

A shot came flat and sharp across the distance. Nat turned. Hays was within range, but the plunging of his mount made accurate aim impossible. Nat snapped off a shot with his hand-gun, then concentrated on keeping the cattle moving. A quarter of an hour later, when the cattle were tiring, Beeton drew up, shouldered his carbine and fired. Hays' horse went end over end, spinning its rider through the air like a cartwheel. Beeton whirled and raced after Nat and Slim.

When the Texan came up where Hays lay, they halted briefly, and one man remained with the downed man while the others continued the pursuit. The cattle were fast tiring now. Nat drew up and looked back. There were only two Texans coming after them. He dismounted, motioned for Beeton to join him, and flagged Eggers on with the herd. As soon as the Texans saw that the two sheriffs meant to make a stand, they slowed, spoke briefly, then rode wide on either side of Nat and Beeton. "Crossfire," the Nevadan said, throwing himself flat upon the hard earth. Suddenly, over the diminishing rumble of the cattle, Nat heard a long, thin scream. He spun around. Charging down upon them was an uneven line of mounted Apaches. Beeton scrambled to his feet with an oath, and the two Texans turned tail without firing a shot, and raced back toward their friend, who was standing beside Hays.

Beeton grabbed his horse and flung himself into the saddle. Nat also mounted, but slower. He was frowning at the lead Indian. As Beeton turned to come up beside him, Nat said, "That's Rawgut."

Some of the Apaches swirled in around the cattle.

Slim spun his horse and raced back toward Nat and Beeton. He was bent low over the saddle, his face contorted by urgency. When the Indians following Rawgut passed the herd, they reined down to a walk. Rawgut threw up his arm, palm outward. Nat returned the gesture, balancing his carbine across his lap with his left hand. Sheriff Beeton exhaled a mighty breath as Slim slid to a halt beside him. "Scared ten years off my life," he said, and his shaken deputy twisted to look back in rigid silence.

When Rawgut was within twenty feet of Nat he halted and motioned back toward the cattle. "Tawnay is satisfied," he said. "Your word is good."

"It almost wasn't," Nat said with relief loud in his voice. "If you hadn't come up, it wouldn't have been."

"You sent word by the soldiers for men to await you at the base of the mountain. We waited. Then we saw the dustcloud and came down to help drive the cattle." Rawgut jutted his chin. "We saw those men shoot at you. We came to help."

"Cussed good thing you did," Sheriff Beeton said, mopping his face. "That's the first time in my life I was ever happy to see Injuns charging at me."

Nat wheeled his horse and made a motion for Rawgut to join him. The Indians fell in beside the white men and journeyed back toward the river crossing, where Hays' Texans were carrying their leader across to the far side. When they saw Nat coming with the Apaches, they left Hays near a willow clump and scattered out to fight. Near the water's edge Nat called out, "You men are under arrest. If you resist I'll let these Apaches stalk you through the willows. Come out unarmed and you won't be harmed."

Only the distant bawling of cattle broke the stillness.

154

Then a cowboy stood up in plain sight with his arms high. "I quit," he said loudly, and walked over where Hays lay. Two more threw down their guns and joined the first man. The last Texan to leave the covert was the leathery man who had kept them under his gun several hours before; he threw his gun down savagely and stalked over beside his friends without looking up.

The lawmen and Rawgut crossed the river and stopped near the Texans. Nat dismounted and knelt beside Hays. The Texan was alive and conscious, eyes dark with hatred. The dewlap he had taken from Nat was lying in the dust beside him, where it had fallen from his pocket. Nat picked it up. "I guess these things don't bring luck after all, do they?" A trickle of blood ran from the edge of Hays' mouth. Beeton got down on both knees and probed the Texan's chest gently. He looked across at Nat and very slowly shook his head. Hays saw the movement and spoke.

"You tryin' to scare me, Sheriff?"

Beeton said he wasn't, and his voice was gentle. "No need to scare you, Hays. I don't know what happened when your horse went down, but you've got a shoulderblade driven down into your lungs."

"You can tell that by feelin'?"

"Yes."

"You fired that shot, damn you!"

"I only meant to get the horse, not you."

"Well," Hays said thickly, "you're a lousy shot. Here, help me sit up."

"You better lie right where you are."

"You go to hell, lawman; I ain't goin' out flat on my back." Hays tried to fight his way to a sitting position. Finally, Nat helped him, and when the Texan was gasping and spitting blood, Nat's arm steadied him.

155

"You lousy Injun-lover," he said to Nat. "If it hadn't been for you I wouldn't be in this fix . . . You and your cussed Apaches!"

"Hays, if you'd given us those cattle like you said you were going to, this wouldn't have happened."

"Go preach in church, you stinkin' lawman—the whole lot of you!" Anger made Hays bleed more. When the pain came he said, "Lay me back down an' keep the sun off." Nat eased him back and shielded his face. "All right, you got your damned cattle, lawman; now let my boys take the rest of the herd down the trail."

"Sure, Hays." Nat got up, holding the dewlap in his fist. Beeton moved closer to the dying man. "Tell me where I've seen you before, Hays."

The Texan's dimming sight brightened briefly and his lips curled down. "Tell you—nothin', lawman!" He shuddered convulsively, and his head dropped to one side. He was dead.

Beeton got up heavily, turned toward the other Texans and asked if they had a shovel in the wagon. They said they had and he sent Slim after it. He went on staring at the dead man. "Somewhere in Nevada, by golly. I know that much."

"It'll come to you," Nat said. He moved over into the shadows, feeling drawn out, and hefting the dewlap idly. Suddenly he stopped toying with the thing and looked hard at it. As Rawgut came up, he threw it up and caught it, and repeated the performance twice more. His eyes widened and he dug into his trouser pocket for a knife, and under Rawgut's interested observation, he slit the dewlap and turned it inside out. *"Beeton, come here!"*

Beeton ambled over and Nat took one of his hands and held it out palm upwards. Beeton looked up, perplexed.

"What's wrong with you, Hendrick?"

Nat ran his thumbnail inside the dewlap and four chunks of raw gold fell onto Beeton's palm. The Nevadan stared stupidly, then he gave a start as though stung. *"Raw gold, Hendrick! That's coarse gold!"* He went weak in the legs and sat down on the hot ground, staring fixedly at the wet, glittering metal in his hand. *"Raw gold; Nevada gold."*

Nat turned to Rawgut. "I want you to save every dewlap off the cattle you butcher," he said. "Do you understand? Every one of them, Rawgut."

"I understand. I will bring them to you tomorrow, Nan. My word is good."

Sheriff Beeton was calling weakly for Eggers. When Slim came up, puzzled and anxious, Beeton held up his hand. "They bought cattle and put it in the dewlaps, Slim. That's how they got that gold out of Nevada without leaving any trace how they done it."

"Huh?"

"Look you idiot; look close. That's Nevada gold if I ever seen any. Here, help me up. Thanks. Nat? Hey, Nat Hendrick, don't let them Injuns touch them cattle."

"Rawgut will bring us the dewlaps, Beeton. He gave me his word."

"His word? Why, there's at least . . ."

"His word's as good as mine. Would you take my word that he'll deliver them tomorrow?"

Beeton fisted his hand around the chunks of gold. He blinked at Nat, then turned and watched the Indians riding back across the river. He said no more, and Nat went among the Texans gathering up their arms. When he was finished. Sheriff Beeton had recovered his composure and walked out to look where the rest of

157

Hays' herd was gazing placidly among the willows. "Nat, we got to get these critters back to Gorman's Crossing and corralled."

"We will," Nat replied, "if you'll quit staring at them long enough to help me tie these Texans on their horses."

"Staring at them?" Beeton said, turning away. "Why, them cattle're worth their weight in gold."

Nat and Beeton returned to Gorman's Crossing with their prisoners and left Slim to watch the cattle. All the way back to town Sheriff Beeton was silent. Not until they were questioning the Texans in Nat's office did some of the astonishment leave him. He cornered the Texan who had held them at gun's point on the landswell that morning and asked where the cattle had come from.

"We bought 'em in Idaho and drove 'em to Nevada," the prisoner said sullenly.

"An' you sewed that gold into them dewlaps in Nevada?"

"That's right."

"And Hays—how did he come by that gold?"

"There're some other fellers worked with us. They got the gold and brought it to us. We done the rest."

"You know the other fellers?"

"Of course I do; I was Hays' foreman."

Beeton sank down on the sofa. "That's nice," he said. "That's real nice. How many in this gold ring?"

"Sixteen, countin' Hays."

"Well, I reckon we can't count him now, since he's buried by the Santa Clara River. You sit down there at that desk, and write me out the names and addresses of them other friends of yours, then we'll start back for Nevada in a day or two." Beeton shoved upright and

158

started for the door. "Be right back," he said to Nat. "I've got to send a telegram to Cedar County. Election time in another month . . ." Sheepy pushed in as Beeton opened the door. He looked angrily at Beeton, then stamped into the office, gazed at the Texans, and turned his eyes on Nat.

"Now then, Sheriff, I'm a patient man," he said with bitterness in his voice, "an' I admire you as a lawman, but I'll be flogged if I'm goin' to cart water t'them cussed Injuns another day."

"Whoa, Sheepy, slow down." Nat grinned down at the irate jailer. "You won't have to. I'm going to take those Indians back to the reservation with me as soon as we get these cowboys locked up."

"That's a promise?"

"It is."

"Here, you galoots, get through that door yonder." Sheepy began pushing the Texans, mumbling profanity under his breath. "Go on, now, doggone you!"

We hope that you enjoyed reading this
Sagebrush Large Print Western.
If you would like to read more Sagebrush titles,
ask your librarian or contact the Publishers:

United States and Canada

Thomas T. Beeler, *Publisher*
Post Office Box 659
Hampton Falls, New Hampshire 03844-0659
(800) 251-8726

United Kingdom, Eire, and
the Republic of South Africa

Isis Publishing Ltd
7 Centremead
Osney Mead
Oxford OX2 0ES England
(01865) 250333

Australia and New Zealand

Australian Large Print Audio & Video P/L
17 Mohr Street
Tullamarine, Victoria, 3043, Australia
1 800 335 364